THE GRAYWOLF SHORT FICTION SERIES

WE ARE NOT IN THIS TOGETHER

STORIES BY
WILLIAM KITTREDGE

EDITED *&* WITH A FOREWORD BY
RAYMOND CARVER

GRAYWOLF PRESS
SAINT PAUL
1984

GRATEFUL ACKNOWLEDGMENT IS DUE THE EDITORS OF THE
FOLLOWING PERIODICALS, IN WHICH THESE STORIES WERE
FIRST PUBLISHED: *Atlantic Monthly, The Iowa Review, Northwest
Review, Ohio Review, Portland Review, Quarry, Sumac,
The Syracuse Scholar & Triquarterly.*

THREE OF THE STORIES INCLUDED IN THIS COLLECTION
WERE PUBLISHED IN *The Van Gogh Fields & Other Stories*
(UNIVERSITY OF MISSOURI PRESS, 1978).

PUBLICATION OF THIS VOLUME IS MADE POSSIBLE IN PART
BY GRANTS FROM THE NATIONAL ENDOWMENT FOR THE ARTS
AND THE WASHINGTON STATE ARTS COMMISSION.

ISBN 0–915308–44–4 (PAPERBACK)
LIBRARY OF CONGRESS CATALOG CARD NUMBER 83–82866

BOOK DESIGN BY SCOTT FREUTEL
TYPESETTING BY IRISH SETTER, PORTLAND

4 6 8 9 7 5 3

Published *by* GRAYWOLF PRESS
POST OFFICE BOX 75006
SAINT PAUL, MINNESOTA
55175

CONTENTS

Foreword

"WHOLE THING WORKS on gravity. Heavy falls and the light floats away." This is said by a wheat rancher as he explains how a threshing machine operates in "The Van Gogh Field," the title story in William Kittredge's first book of short stories. *Heavy falls and the light floats away.* And, a little later on in the same story: "What you do matters. What you do, right or wrong, has consequences, brother." This is true in "real-life" situations as well as in the "life-like" situations given to us by the best writers of fiction. *What you do matters.* Listen up: the stories included in *We Are Not in This Together* are wonderfully rendered pieces about a special and particular place in this country that has not had that many writers speaking for it up to now. Wallace Stegner comes to mind. And H. L. Davis and Walter van Tilburg Clark. More recently Max Schott, John Keeble, Jim Welch, Tom McGuane. With this new collection, William Kittredge secures his place.

The West is a far country, indeed, but the West portrayed in these stories is not the West as in *West Coast*; cities like San Francisco, Portland, Seattle; these cities, for all the influence they exert on the lives of Kittredge's people, may as well be on the European mainland. The West in these stories runs from Red Bluff in north central California, through eastern Oregon into Idaho, Montana, and Wyoming. Drawing from the small towns and glens, tourist courts and spent farms, the author gives us characters who are light-years away from the American Dream, characters whose high hopes have broken down on them and gotten left behind like old, abandoned combines.

Kittredge knows the weather up there in his country, inside

and out. And the barometer is dropping fast; a man could get hurt, a man could get killed. They die, some of the people, of alcohol poisoning; or they break through ice on a hunting trip and drown, or burn to death in a car, drunk and sleeping beside the highway. Or they're killed by a strange kid "gone rotten" as in the long story, "The Soap Bear," a brilliant, virtuoso piece of writing that puts me in mind of William Gass's "The Pedersen Kid" for its demonic intensity and its vivid depiction of a place. Listen to what follows. How would you like to have this kid in your house, with the drop on you, after he's committed murder five times over?

> "Your feet get cold, you put on your hat. There's a rule. Your head is like a refrigerator, so you have to turn it off to get your fingers and toes warm. So you put on your hat." He got up and went into the hallway where his stocking cap was stuffed into the pocket of his sheepskin coat, and pulled the cap down over his wet hair. "Now," he said, "I don't feel no pain, because my head is covered. You got to do lots of things this way, with your head turned off."

Here are some of the places that figure in these stories: Vacaville, Nyall, Arlington, Horn Creek, Black Flat, Frenchglen, Mary's River, Corvallis, Prineville, Manteca, Davanero, Bakersfield, Shafter, Salem, Yakima, Paiute Creek, Klamath Falls, Tracy, Walla Walla, Donan, Red Bluff, McDermit, Denio, Walker Lake, Bitterroot, Cody, Elk River, Clark Fork, Lompoc, Colorado Springs.

Some names: Clyman Teal, Robert Ohnter, Jules Russel, Ambrose Vega, Davy Horse ("so called after his right leg was crushed against a rock solid juniper gatepost by a stampeding green colt he tried to ride one Sunday morning when he was drunk, showing off for women"), Ben Alton, Corrie Alton, Steffanie Rudd, Jerome Bedderly, Oralie York, Red Yount, Lonnie, Cleve, Big Jimmy and "his running pal, Clarence Dunes," Virgil and Mac Banta, Sheriff Shirley Holland, his wife, Doris, Billy Kumar who is "dumber than rocks," Marly

Prester, Amos Frantz who "kept a whore from Butte whose name was Annie," Dora and Slipper Count.

There's poetry in the naming of these places and people, but little of it in the lives of the characters who figure in Kittredge's stories. Maybe there was a little, once, in the beginning, but then something happened — it was worked out of you, or beaten out of you, or you drank too much, too long, and it left you; and now you're worse off than ever because you still have to go through the motions, even though you know it's for nothing now, a senseless reminder of better days. Now, no matter what, even if your brother is being buried that day, killed in a barroom brawl, you still have to go out and feed the stock. If you don't feed them, they won't be fed. You have to do it. There are obligations. And maybe this same brother, you've just found out, is the father of the child your wife is carrying. This is going to take some getting used to, adjustments are going to have to be made. This is from "Thirty-Four Seasons of Winter," one of the finest stories in the book.

If the characters listen to music, it's music by Waylon Jennings, Roger Miller, Loretta Lynn, Tom T. Hall singing "Spokane Motel Blues," Merle Haggard, Linda Ronstadt and "Party Doll"; church music like "Rock of Ages" and "Nearer My God to Thee." If they read anything at all, they read *The Sporting News*. Besides, where most of them live, the big city newspapers, the papers from Seattle or Spokane or Portland or San Francisco are a day late getting there, and so the gloomy horoscopes are a confirmation rather than a prediction.

There's God's plenty of "dis-ease" in these stories, a phrase Camus used to describe a certain terrible kind of domesticity. Listen to Shirley Holland, the middle-aged sheriff in "The Soap Bear," a childless man in his twentieth year of marriage:

> How do you enter your own house when something has gone bad on the inside, when it doesn't seem like your place to live any more, when you almost cannot recall living there although it was the place where you mostly

ate and slept for all your grownup life? Try to remember two or three things about living there. Try to remember cooking one meal. . . . Sometimes there is no choice but to walk into your own house. . . . There is the moment when you walk in and take a look in your house, like any traveler.

"When I grew up," the kid said, "you knew my father. His name was Mac Banta, down there in the Bitterroot."

"I never knew anybody named Banta," Holland said.

"Well, he was there anyway," the kid said. "And there was those spring mornings with the geese flying north and I would stand out on the lawn with the sun just coming up and the fence painted white around my mother's roses and it would be what my father called a bluebird morning. My sister would be there, and my mother and my father, and the birds playing in the lilac. Comes down to a world of hurt was what my father would say, and he would laugh because nothing could hurt you on those bluebird mornings."

William Kittredge writes about the West, about his world and its inhabitants, with pity and terror and love. I think his work is singular and unforgettable.

RAYMOND CARVER

WE ARE NOT IN THIS TOGETHER

The Waterfowl Tree

THEY RAN INTO SNOW almost two hours before reaching the valley, the storm at twilight whipping in gusts across the narrow asphalt. The station wagon moved slowly through the oncoming darkness.

"A long haul," his father said. "Eva will be wondering."

The boy, tall and seventeen, his hands behind his neck, watched out the glazed and crusted side windows at the indeterminate light. This mention of the woman could be a signal, some special beginning.

"Is she pretty? he asked.

"Pretty enough for me. And that's pretty enough."

The man laughed and kept his eyes on the road. He was massive, a widower in his late fifties. "I've got too old for worrying about pretty," he said. "All I want is gentle. When that's all you want, you got to be getting old."

In a little while, the man said, "I remember hunting when I was a kid. It was different then, more birds for one thing, and you had to kill something with every shot."

"How do you mean?" the boy asked.

"We were meat hunters. You spent money for shells, you brought home meat. I saw Teddy Spandau die on that account. Went off into open water chest deep, just trying to get some birds he shot. Cramped up and drowned. We hauled a boat down and fished him out that afternoon."

The snow began to thin and the man pushed the car faster and concentrated on his driving.

"It was like this then," he said. "Snowing, and ice a foot thick and below zero all day."

The boy wished his father would go on talking about these far-away and unsuspected things. But the man, long estranged from this remote and misted valley of his childhood, sat hunched over the wheel, absorbed in the road and grimacing.

"I guess it was different in those days," the boy said, wanting his father to keep talking.

"Quite a bit different," the man answered. "A different life altogether."

After this they drove in silence. It was completely dark when they came out of the storm, driving through the last drifting flakes into the light of a full moon and an intense and still cold that made the new snow crystallize and occasionally sparkle in the headlights.

"Freeze solid by morning," the man said. "Be some new birds coming in."

He stopped the car and switched off the headlights.

"Look there," he said, pointing.

The boy cranked down his window and looked across the distorted landscape of snow, blue and subdued in the moonlight. Far away he saw a high ridge shadowed in darkness.

"That's the rim," his father said. "We'll be home directly."

The boy looked again at the black fault. How could this be home, this place under that looming wall?

"All my life," the man said, "in strange places, I've caught myself looking up and expecting to see that rim."

The long attic room, unfinished, raftered under the peak roof, filled with soft darkness, illuminated by blue softness where moonlight shone through windows on either end. On the floor and inward sloping east wall he could see light reflected up from downstairs. The boy lay in the bundled warmth of a mummy bag on an iron cot and watched the light, imagined that he could see it slowly climb the wall as the moon dropped. The cold in this shed-like room above the barn was complete and still and frosted his breath when he moved.

"You're young and tough," his father had said. "You draw

the outdoor room."

They'd unloaded the boy's suitcase and the new gear quickly in the darkness, tried to be quiet because the house across the road was completely dark. Then his father went ahead with a flashlight and they carried the gear up an old flight of stairs at the side of the barn and pushed through the ancient hanging door that opened into this long, barren room. After unrolling the sleeping bag on the cot, his father gripped him by the shoulder and shone the light in his face.

"You'll be warm inside the bag," the man said. "Take your coat in with you and sleep with your clothes on. That way they won't be frozen in the morning. Stick the boots under you. We'll get you up for breakfast."

Then he turned and took the light and left the boy standing in the cold. What would greet his father in that dark house across the road? They'd come upon the place after rounding a curve in the gravel road that crossed the upper part of the valley. A bunch of trees and a house and a barn and some corrals; just that in the midst of unending fields of fenced snow.

The boots made a comforting hump and the boy curled around them and tried to warm himself. Suddenly he was frantic and wished he were back in his bed at school, enduring the vacation, trying to guess tomorrow's movie.

"Goddamn," he said, clenched and shaking. "Damn, dirty son of a bitch."

But the warmth came and with it a quiet numbness. He felt himself drift and then he slept, surprised that he was not going to lie awake and search for a sense of how it would be in the morning.

And now, just as quickly, he was awake and watching the slow light on the far wall. Then he recognized, almost unnoticed among his thoughts, an ancient crying. Coyotes. He smiled and huddled deep in his warmth, secure against the night. The calls came fine and clear, and he struggled to get an arm out of the warmth. He looked at the illuminated face of his watch. It was almost three o'clock.

The wailing stopped and there was silence.

Geese were flying. He could hear, far away, but still clear and distinct, their wandering call. He felt himself slipping again into peaceful sleep. Then the coyotes began a long undulating wail and small yipping. He rested his head on his arm and slept, lulled by their noise and a small rhythm of his own.

A hand shook him, gently and firmly, and for a moment he was elsewhere and lost, then he was awake and remembering. He pushed up from the warmth of the sleeping bag and looked out at the morning, at the smile of this strange woman and the frosted windows, and the rough shingle and rafter roof. His breath swirled softly in the cold morning air. He smiled at the woman and stretched his arms. The woman stood next to his bed, leaning over, one hand touching him through the layers of the sleeping bag.

"Welcome," she said. "On the coldest day in a thousand years."

Really nothing but a fuzzy-headed woman. She was bundled in hunting clothes and wore a down cap tied under her chin with fringes and curls of hair protruding. Not the woman he'd expected. The face was heavier and older than he would have imagined, and he suddenly understood that his father was almost an old man.

"You must be Eva."

"The same," she said. "The famous Eva. Come on, breakfast is almost ready."

"I can't." He grinned, surprised at her easiness, taken in spite of himself. "I don't have any pants on."

"Come on. I won't look if I can help myself." She pulled on his arm and grinned.

He scrambled out of bed and was shocked at the cold. He jumped in dismay when she grabbed one of his bare ankles with her cold hands. He escaped and she dropped the mittens she had tucked under one arm and began rummaging in the bed, fishing in the warm darkness, finally pulling out his pants and coat while he wrapped his arms around himself and watched. "Get 'em on," she said.

The area between the house and the barn was ankle-deep in new snow and marked only by the boot tracks of the night before and her footprints of this morning. The trees around the house were heaped with ice and snow. He had to squint against the glare.

The house was rough and worn and old, without any rugs to cover the plank floor and with homemade wooden chairs and a long table with benches on either side. The boy stood in the doorway and felt with pleasure the shock of warm air that softened his face. In one corner of this main room was a big wood stove with chopped wood and kindling in a box beside it. His father sat on a stool beside the stove, filling shell belts. Open shell boxes were scattered around him on the floor.

"Come on in," the man said. "Close the door. Charlie will have breakfast on in a minute."

Through an open doorway on the far side of the room came the reflection of morning sunlight. Through the doorway he could see another smaller man working over a woodburning cook stove. The woman began pulling off her cap and coat, piling them on the far end of the table. No one, not even the woman, paid attention to the water and melting ice on the floor.

"Holy smokes," the woman said, brushing her hair back and tucking her shirt in her pants. "It's so damned cold out there he could have froze."

"Make you tough, won't it boy." His father looked up at him.

"It wasn't bad," the boy said. "I stayed warm."

"That's the spirit." The man stood up, dropping the finished shell belts from his lap to the floor. "Come on."

The boy followed him into the next room where the other man was tending a frying pan full of eggs and another pan with bacon. "This is Charlie Anderson," his father said. "Me and

Charlie are hunting partners. From the old days."

Charlie turned and shook hands with the boy. "Glad to have you, son," he said. "Eat in a minute." Charlie nodded and went back to his cooking.

"Come here." His father, massive in boots and khaki hunting gear, walked to the far end of the kitchen and opened a door to the outside. The boy followed him out, and the cold was at him again, hard and stiff.

"Look at that," his father said. Behind the house was a small orchard of six or seven trees. The tree nearest the house, gnarled and holding stiff winter limbs towards the thin sky, was hung with dead geese and ducks. They were in bunches of a dozen or more, strung together on short pieces of rope and suspended from heavy nails driven into limbs, crusted with ice and frozen and absolutely still, frosted and sparkling in the light.

"Deep freeze," the man said. "We hung them like that when we were kids."

The boy supposed that he should say something to please his father but was not sure what that would be. He turned away from the tree and looked to the west where the winter rim he had seen in the moonlight rose high over the far edge of the valley. Through the still air he could define individual trees among the groves of juniper along its upper edge. He heard the geese calling again and looked to see them flying, distant and wavering, and remembered the night before. "They sound so far away," he said.

"We'll get after them," his father said. "As soon as we eat."

The boy turned and looked again at the tree, hung with dead birds. He was unable to feel anything beyond his own chill.

"We hung them there when I was a kid," his father said. "A man named Basston owned this place, and my old man would bring me down here to help out on the weekends. There'd be a crowd all season. Guys from the city. Basston died. The guys stopped coming. Let's eat."

The boy watched his father turn and go in, surprised at the

life that had been his father's. Maybe that's why he brought me here, he thought. To let me see what he was.

"Coming," he said.

The boy huddled lower in the blind of tules and reeds and wished the birds would hurry and come again. He and his father sat hidden only a few yards from a small patch of open water, on a neck of land in the tule swamps of the valley. They were alone and a long way from the warmth of the station wagon.

"I'll take you with me," the man said when they first spotted the birds with field glasses. He pointed far off from where they were parked above the frozen swamp, and the boy saw them, milling and keeping a stirred bit of water open and free of ice. A fantastic sight through the glasses – thousands of ducks crowding in the water and great bunches of Honkers and lesser Canadians walking the ice around them.

"Eva and Charlie can go over and wait at the decoys," his father said. "Give us two shots at them."

No one said anything, and after straightening the tangled gear in the back of the station wagon, the four of them walked off, two in each direction. The boy and his father walked in a long arc around the birds in order to come up on them from the sheltered land side and get as close as possible before they flushed. "Lots of time," his father said, after they'd walked a half mile or so. He was panting and sweating in the heavy gear. "Give Eva and Charlie time to get over to the decoys."

And their stalk was a good one. Between them, they had five greenhead Mallard drakes and two hens. "Pick the greenheads," his father whispered before they came up shooting. "Pick one each time before you shoot."

The geese had been too wise and flushed early, taking a few ducks with them, but the main flock of ducks was almost too easy, standing nearly still in the air during the long and suddenly clamorous second as they flushed, rising in waves, time to reload and shoot again before they were gone. The boy's first two shots had simply been pulled off into the rising mass.

Then he remembered his father's words and aimed carefully and selectively.

After the first flush, the man and the boy dropped into the tules near the water's edge, leaving the dead birds on the ice. The thousands of ducks grouped and then turned in the distance and came back at them in long whirring masses, sensing something and veering off before getting into shooting range, but filling the air with the mounting rush of their wings. The boy, awed nearly to tears by the sight above him, and the sound of the wings, sat concealed beside his father and was unable and unready to shoot again.

"Charlie and I used to hunt here when we were kids," the man said after a time, during a lull. "This is the real coming back. I remember waking in the spring when the birds were flying north. I could hear them from my bed, and I'd go out and stand on the knoll behind the house and watch them leave and hear them calling and smell the corrals and just look at the valley where it had turned green and then over at the rim where a little snow lay near the top. I guess those were the best days I ever lived." The man spoke softly, and the boy half-listened to him and sucked in his breath, waiting for the birds to come wheeling at them again, thinking the sound of their flight the most beautiful thing he had ever heard.

Then the birds stopped coming, and he and his father went out on the ice and gathered the dead ones, five beautiful greenheads and the two hens and carried them back to the hiding place. "The dead ones scared them off," his father said. "Now we'll have to wait awhile on the honkers."

And so they waited, the boy trying to be comfortable in his heavy clothing as he listened to his father.

"We used to haul the birds back to the house in a wagon. There was ten times as many in those days and lots of Canvasbacks and Redheads. You don't see those birds any more." The man moved quietly and easily around their nest, pulling reeds together over them until they were completely hidden.

"I remember one afternoon when the wind was blowing and

the clouds were below the rim and we sat in one place, Charlie and me, fourteen years old I guess, and we shot up over a case of old man Basston's 12-gauge shells. The birds kept coming and we just kept shooting. We killed a hundred and fifty birds that one afternoon. It was almost night when we got back to camp and we hung those birds in the dark and old man Basston came out and we stood under that tree and he gave each of us a couple of drinks of the best bourbon whiskey on earth and sent us to bed like men. I guess that was the best day, the tops in my life."

Had everything been downhill since? The boy understood, or hoped that he did, why he was here, that his father was trying to make up, to present a view of life before the time had completely passed. Was this only for himself, he wondered? He listened to his father and thought of this woman, Eva, and the others and the different man his father had become to him in this place.

Eventually the geese came, very high and veered out in their great formations. They dropped and started to wheel when they saw the water.

The flocks seemed endless, long flights coming one before the next, circling and wheeling and dropping. "I'll tell you when," the man said. "Just lay quiet."

The first flight had landed and was calming itself in the water and on the edge of the ice when the next, under a larger flight of ducks, came directly over them, settled on stiff wings, fell directly towards the water, unconscious and intent. "Now," the man said, and they rose, waist deep in the tules, and shot three times each and dropped six birds easily, the huge black and white geese thudding on the ice.

"That's it," his father said. "Beautiful shooting. Enough for this day. Let's go. They'll be back."

The geese scattered and wheeled above them while they went out on the ice again and began to pick up the dead birds. They were heavy and beautiful birds and the boy twisted their necks the way his father did and felt sorry that they could not have lived and yet was glad that they were dead. They were trophies of this world, soft and heavy and dead birds.

"We'll sit around this afternoon and play some fourhanded gin," his father said, after they had gathered the birds. "You ever play gin?"

"Sure," the boy said. "For pennies and buttons." They strung the ducks on a short piece of rope and the geese on another. "You carry the ducks," his father said. "I'll bring the geese. We'll go back across the ice."

It was a mile across to where the station wagon sat on a knoll. The going was slick and tricky with the new snow on the ice. The boy walked gingerly at first, then faster. Soon he was well out ahead of his father. The man came slowly and solidly, breathing heavily.

Far away the rim was a sharply defined edge. Between him and that high point, the boy watched the flocks of birds, some clearly visible against the flat sky, others almost indistinguishable against the snow-covered slopes.

From behind him he heard a distant, muffled cry.

He turned and saw that his father was gone, vanished from sight. Then the man reappeared on the surface of the snow, floundering in the water. The boy dropped the shotgun and the birds and ran towards his father.

While running he saw the man raise himself violently and wave, shout, then fall back again.

The cry, the boy understood, was a command to stay back; but he ran on, slipping and falling towards the hole in the ice. The man floundered through the chest-deep water, while the geese on their little rope floated beside him. The water steamed. The ice, incredibly, was soft and only a few inches thick.

The man waved him back and the boy stopped, yards short of the edge. He watched his father for some sign of what had happened, what to do.

The man stood quietly in the steaming and putrid water,

gasping. He had been completely submerged and now the water was under his armpits. "Stay there," his father said, beginning to shake. "There's a hot spring and the ice is rotten."

"Let me rest a little," he said. "Then I'll try to work my way over to the solid ice."

The boy stood helpless. The edges of the broken and jagged water had begun to freeze again, solidifying as he watched. "Can you stand it?"

"It's not so bad here," the man said, composed now and shaking less, speaking quietly. "But it'll be cold out there."

Then the man began to move again, working slowly, pulling each leg out of the deep bottom mud and then moving forward another step. He made it almost to the edge of the ice and then stopped. "God Almighty," he said. "It's so goddamned cold."

And then the boy heard his father mutter something else, something subdued and private, saw his face begin to collapse and draw into itself and grow distant. The man began to thrash and move forward in lunges, reaching toward the edge of the ice, fighting and gasping, moving toward the boy.

Then, his eyes on the boy, the man simply turned onto his back, eyes rolling back and becoming blank. Then he sank, flailing his arms, the birds entangled in the rope going down with him. Then there was nothing but the water and some bubbling.

And then there were no bubbles, nothing but the dead geese floating quietly, their heads pulled under the surface by the rope that still encircled his father's body.

The boy heard again the distant honking of the geese and the whirring of wings as a pair of ducks came directly at him and suddenly swung away.

The boy turned and began to rush across the ice, scrambling and slipping, sometimes falling as he ran across the open ice toward the station wagon.

Back in the station wagon with the engine going and the heater turned on, he began to shake. He stretched out on the seat and fell out of himself like a stone into what might have been taken for sleep.

He awoke fully in the warm darkness of a completely strange and unknown room, wondering what place this was. And then, with terrible swiftness, he was again in the moment of the inexplicable thing that had happened – he saw his father's eyes rolling backwards. He knew that it had happened, understood that this was one of the bedrooms in the strange house. He put his feet on the floor and was surprised to find himself in his underwear. A door slammed in another part of the house and he heard a voice, Eva's voice.

"I wonder if he's still sleeping?"

She appeared in the dim doorway.

"He's awake," she said over her shoulder.

She came into the room and turned on the light. Her hair was brushed away from her face and fell in waves to her shoulders. She looked younger, he thought, and somehow out of place here. He pulled the sheets over his bare legs.

"I'm all right now," he said. "Did they get him out?"

"He is out." The woman spoke formally and slowly, showing, the boy thought, that they were still really strangers, after all. "And now it is night. You slept a long time."

The boy turned away, beginning to cry, dissolving into the terror once more. The woman snapped off the light and came across the room to him. "Try to rest," she said, "I'm going to bed now.

"Your father loved this place," the woman said. "He told me it was the only surely happy place in his life. I'll be back in a minute," Eva said, and left the room.

The only surely happy place.

Presently the woman returned, wearing a brocade robe that reached the floor and with her hair pulled back and knotted behind her head. The boy turned and looked at her in the dim light, saw her drop the robe and pull back the covers on the other side of the bed and get under the covers, flinching when she touched the sheets. The boy started to get up.

"Stay and we'll talk," she said. She took him by the arm and pulled him towards her, and he was again surprised at the coldness of her hands.

"Why?" he said. "Why did it happen?" He began to cry again.

"His heart," she said. "He had been having trouble." The woman moved closer to him and put her arm around his shoulders. "I'm sorry," she said. "God," she said.

Presently he slept again, exhausted and calmed, slowly moving to huddle against the warmth of the woman. In the middle of the night he woke and felt the woman shuddering and crying beside him.

He woke to warmth and sunlight coming through the open doorway of the room. He was alone in the bed.

In the outer room the woman and Charlie Anderson were sitting quietly at the table. "Sit down," Charlie said. "I'll get you some food."

"Charlie doesn't trust my cooking," the woman said. The woman went into the kitchen and returned with a mug of coffee. She seemed self-conscious and almost shy.

Charlie Anderson came from the kitchen with eggs and a thick slice of fried ham. "Eat good," he said to the boy.

"He will," the woman said.

The boy wondered where the grief had gone and if his father had been so easily dismissed.

"We seen the end of a fine man," Charlie Anderson said and began to remove the dishes.

So the boy ate and watched them, these strangers. And then he walked through the house uneasily and went out through the kitchen door and stood beneath the heavily laden tree and shuffled in the snow and fingered the frozen bark while looking again to the far-off rim.

Eva came outside. The boy was conscious of her standing silently behind him. He blinked in the radiance and watched the high-flying birds, geese moving to feed and water. He heard the woman make a sound behind him, and he turned to see her face crumpling. She gasped slightly. She moved to him and pressed herself against him while she shook and wept. He stood with his arms at his sides and felt the softness of her breasts behind the sweater, and then nothing but the cold in her hair which was loose and open against his face.

Then she was quiet.

"Let's go in," she said. "I'm cold."

She moved away and he followed her, oblivious to everything and completely drawn into himself.

"It will make you tough," his father had said.

"Goddamn you for this," the boy thought.

He slammed the door behind him and went to stand before the fire. The woman stood at the window with her hands behind her while Charlie Anderson busied himself with the dishes. The house seemed filled with the musk of the dead birds. The boy's numb fingers throbbed and ached as he held them open to the radiant warmth of the fire. "Goddamn everything," the boy said.

Thirty-Four Seasons of Winter

BEN ALTON REMEMBERED YEARS in terms of winter. Summers all ran together, each like the last, heat and baled hay and dust. "That was '59," he'd say. "The year I wintered in California." He'd be remembering manure-slick alleys of a feedlot outside Manteca, a flat horizon and constant rain.

Or flood years. "March of '64, when the levees went." Or open winters. "We fed cattle the whole of February in our shirt-sleeves. For Old Man Swarthout." And then he'd be sad. "One week Art helped. We was done every day by noon and drunk by three." Sad because Art was his step-brother and dead, and because there'd been nothing but hate between them when Art was killed.

Ben and Art fought only once, when they were thirteen. Ben's father, Corrie Alton, moved in with Art's old lady on her dry-land place in the hills north of Davanero, and the boys bunked together in a back room. The house was surrounded by a fenced dirt yard where turkeys picked, shaded by three withering peach trees; and the room they shared was furnished with two steel-frame cots and a row of nails where they hung what extra clothing they owned. The first night, while the old people were drinking in town, the boys fought. Ben took a flattened nose and chipped tooth against one of the cot frames and was satisfied and didn't try again.

The next year Art's mother sold the place for money to drink on, and when that was gone Ben's old man pulled out, heading for Shafter, down out of Bakersfield, going to see friends and work a season in the spuds. Corrie never came back or sent word, so the next spring the boys took a job setting siphons for an onion farmer, doing the muddy and exhausting work of one man, supporting themselves and Art's mother. She died the spring they were seventeen; and Art began to talk about getting out of town, fighting in the ring, being somebody.

So he ran every night, and during the day he and Ben stacked alfalfa bales, always making their thousand a day, twenty bucks apiece, and then in the fall Art went to Portland and worked out in a gym each afternoon, learning to fight, and spent his evenings swimming at the YMCA or watching movies. Early in the winter he began to get some fights; and for at least the first year he didn't lose. People began to know his name in places like Salem and Yakima and Klamath Falls.

He fought at home only once, a January night in the Peterson barn on the edge of town, snow falling steadily. The barn warmed slowly, losing its odor of harness leather and rotting hay; and under the circle of lights which illumintaed the fighters in a blue glare, country people smoked and bet and drank. Circling a sweating and tiring Mexican boy, Art tapped his gloves and brushed back his thin blond hair with a quick forearm, sure and quiet. Then he moved under an overhand right, ducking in a quick new way he must have learned in Portland; and then he was inside, forcing, and flat on his feet, grunting as he followed each short chop with his body. The Mexican backed against one of the rough juniper posts supporting the ring, covered his face, gloves fumbling together as he began sinking and twisting, knees folding; and it ended with the Mexican sprawled and cut beneath one eye, bleeding from the nose, and Art in his corner, breathing easily while he flexed and shook his arms as if he weren't loose yet. Art spit the white mouthpiece onto the wet, gray canvas and ducked away under the ropes.

That night, Ben sat in the top row of the little grandstand and watched two men drag the other fighter out of the ring and attempt to revive him by pouring water over his head. Ben hugged his knees and watched the crowd settle and heard the silence while everybody watched. Finally the Mexican boy shook his head and sat up, and the crowd moved in a great sigh.

The next summer Art showed up with Clara, brought her back with him from a string of fights in California. It was an August afternoon, dead hot in the valley hayfields, and dust rose in long spirals from the field ahead where five balers were circling slowly, eating windrows of loose hay and leaving endless and uniform strings of bales. Ben was working the stack, unloading trucks, sweating through his pants every day before noon, shirtless and peeling.

The lemon-colored Buick convertible came across the stubble, bouncing and wheeling hard, just ahead of its own dust, and stopped twenty or thirty yards from the stack. Art jumped out holding a can of beer over his head. The girl stood beside the convertible in the dusty alfalfa stubble and squinted into the glaring light, moist and sleepy-looking. She was maybe twenty, and her sleeveless white blouse was wrinkled from sleeping in the car and sweat-gray beneath the arms. But she was blond and tan and direct in the one-hundred-degree heat of the afternoon. "Ain't she something?" Art said. "She's a kind of prize I brought home." He laughed and slapped her on the butt.

"Hello, Ben," she said. "Art told me about you." They drank a can of beer, iced and metallic tasting, and Art talked about the fighting in California, Fresno, and Tracy, and while he talked he ran his fingers slowly up and down Clara's bare arm. Ben crouched in the shade of the convertible with his beer and tried not to watch the girl. That night he lay awake and thought about her, and everything about that meeting seemed too large and real, like some memory of childhood.

Anyway, she was living and traveling with Art. Then the fall he was twenty-five, fighting in Seattle, Art broke his right hand in a way that couldn't be fixed and married Clara and came home to live, driving a logging truck in the summer and drink-

ing in the bars and drawing his unemployment through the
winters, letting Clara work as a barmaid when they were
broke. The years got away until one afternoon in a tavern
called The Tarpaper Shack, when Ben and Art were thirty-one.
Art was sitting with a girl named Marie, and when Ben came in
and wandered over to the booth she surprised him by being
quiet and nice, with brown eyes and dark hair, not the kind Art
ran with on his drunks; and by the end of the summer Marie
and Ben were engaged.

Which caused no trouble until Christmas. The stores were
open late, but the streets with their decorations were deserted,
looking like a carnival at four in the morning, lighted and
ready to tear down and move.

"You gonna marry that pig?" Art said. Art was drunk. The
barkeeper, a woman called Virgie, was leaning on the counter.

"I guess I am," Ben said. "But don't sweat it." Then he noticed Virgie looking past them to the far corner of the vaulted
room. A worn row of booths ran there, beyond the lighted
shuffleboard table and bowling machine. Above the last booth
he saw the shadowed back of Clara's head. Just the yellow hair
and yet certainly her. Art was grinning.

"You see her," he said talking to Ben. "She's got a problem.
She ain't getting any."

Ben finished the beer and eased the glass back to the wooden
counter, wishing he could leave, wanting no more of their
trouble. Clara was leaning back, eyes closed and the table in
front of her empty except for her clasped hands. She didn't
move or look as he approached.

"Hello, Clara," he said. And when she opened her eyes it
was the same, like herons over the valley swamps, white
against green. Even tired she looked good. "All right if I sit?"
he asked. "You want a beer?"

She sipped from his, taking the glass without speaking,
touching his hand with her hand, then smiling and licking the

froth from her lips. "Okay," she said, and he ordered another glass and sat down beside her.

"How you been?" he said. "All right?"

"You know," she said, looking sideways at him, never glancing toward Art. "You got a pretty good idea how I been." Then she smiled. "I hear you're getting married."

"Just because you're tied up," he said, and she grinned again, more like her old self now. "I mean it," he said. "Guess I ought to tell you once."

"Don't," she said. "For Christ sake. Not with that bastard over there laughing." She drank a little more of the beer. "I mean it," she said, after a moment. "Leave me alone."

Ben picked up his empty glass and walked toward the bar, turning the glass in his hand and feeling how it fit his grasp. He stood looking at the back of Art's head, the thin hair, fine and blond; and then he wrapped the glass in his fist and smashed it into the hollow of Art's neck, shattering the glass and driving Art's face into the counter. Then he ran, crashing out the door and onto the sidewalk.

His hand was cut and bleeding. He picked glass from his palm and wrapped his hand in his handkerchief as he walked, looking in the store windows, bright and lighted for Christmas.

Clara left for Sacramento that night, lived there with her father, worked in a factory southeast of town, making airplane parts and taking care of the old man, not coming back until he died. Sometimes Ben wondered if she would have come back anyway, even if the old man hadn't died. Maybe she'd just been waiting for Art to come after her. And then one day on the street he asked, "You and Art going back together?" just hoping he could get her to talk awhile.

"I guess not," she said. "That's what he told me."

"I'm sorry," Ben said. And he was.

"I came back because I wanted," she said. "Guess I lived here too long."

That spring Ben and Marie were married and began living out of town, on a place her father owned; and the next fall his father was killed, crushed under a hillside combine in Washington, just north of Walla Walla, drunk and asleep at the leveling wheel, dead when they dug him out. And then the summer Art and Ben turned thirty-four Marie got pregnant and that winter Art was killed, shot in the back of the head by a girl named Steffanie Rudd, a thin red-haired girl just out of high school and, so people said, knocked up a little. Art was on the end stool in The Tarpaper Shack, his usual place, when the girl entered quietly and shot before anyone noticed. He was dead when he hit the floor, face destroyed, blood splattered over the mirror and glasses behind the bar. And all the time music he'd punched was playing on the jukebox. *Trailer for sale or rent*; and, *I can't stop loving you*; and, *Time to bum again*; and *That's what you get for loving me*: Roger Miller, Ray Charles, Waylon Jennings.

Ben awakened the night of the shooting and heard Marie on the phone, felt her shake him awake in the dim light of the bedroom. She seemed enormously frightened and continued to shake him, as if to awaken herself. She was eight months pregnant.

"He's dead." She spoke softly, seeming terrified, as if some idea she feared had been at last confirmed. "He never had a chance," she said.

"He had plenty." Ben sat up and put his arm around her, forced from his shock.

"They never gave him anything." She bent over and began to cry.

Later, it nearly morning, after coffee and cigarettes, when Marie gave up and went to bed, Ben sat alone at the kitchen table. "Afraid of everything," Art had said. "That's how they are. Every stinking one."

Ben saw Art drunk and talking like he was ready for anything, actually involved with nothing except for a string of girls like the one who shot him. And then, somehow, the idea of Art and Marie got hold of Ben. It came from the way she had cried and carried on about Art. There was something wrong. Sitting there at the table, feeling the knowledge seep around his defenses, Ben knew what it was. He got up from the chair.

She was in the bedroom, curled under the blankets, crying softly. "What is it?" he asked. "There's something going on." She didn't open her eyes, but the crying seemed to slow a little. Ben waited, standing beside the bed, looking down, all the time wondering, as he became more sure, if it had happened in this bed, and all the time knowing it made no difference where it happened. And it was her fault. Not any fault of Art's. Art was what he was. She could have stopped him. Ben's hands felt strange, as if there was something to be done he couldn't recognize. He asked again, hearing his voice harsh and strained. "What is it? Marie?"

She didn't answer. He forced her onto her back and held her there, waiting for her to open her eyes while she struggled silently, twisting her upper body against his grip. His fingers sank into her shoulder and his wrist trembled. They remained like that, forcing against each other. Then she relaxed and opened her eyes. "What is it?" he asked again. "It was something between you and Art, wasn't it?"

Her eyes were changed, shielded. She shook her head. "No," she said. "No."

"He was screwing you, wasn't he? Is it his kid?"

"It was a long time ago," she said.

"My ass." He let go of her shoulder. "That's why you're so tore up. Because you ain't getting any more from him." He walked around the bed, unable for some reason, because of what he was left with, to ask her if it happened here, in this bed. "Isn't that right?" he said. "How come you married me? He turn you down?"

"Because I was afraid of him. I didn't want him. He was just fooling. I wanted you, not him."

Ben slapped her, and she curled quickly again, her hands

pressed to her mouth, crying, shoulders hunching. He made her face him. "You ain't getting away," he said. "So I was a nice tame dog, and you took me."

"You'll hurt the baby."

"His goddamned baby!"

"It all broke off when I met you," she said. "He told me to go ahead, that you'd be good to me." It had surprised him when they met that she was with Art, but somehow he'd never until now gotten the idea they had anything going on. "It was only a few times after I knew you," she said. "He begged me."

"So I got stuck with the leavings." He cursed her again, at the same time listening to at least a little of what she said. "He begged me." That was sad. Remembering Art those last years, after he came home to stay, Ben believed her.

"So he dumped you off onto me," Ben said. "I wish I could thank him."

"It wasn't like that. He loved you. He said for me to marry you and be happy."

"So you did. And I was stupid enough to go for it."

"He was a little boy. It was fun, but he was a little boy."

"I'm happy," Art said, "things worked out so nice for you." She shook her head and didn't answer. Ben wondered what he should do. It was as if he had never been married, had been right in always imagining his life as single. He'd watched his friends settle, seen their kids start to grow up, and it had seemed those were things he was not entitled to, that he was going to grow old in a habit of taverns, rented rooms, separate from the married world. And now he was still there, outside. And she'd kept it all a secret. "You stinking pig," he said slowly.

"Ben, it was a long time ago. Ben."

He was tired and his work was waiting. Maybe it was a long time ago and maybe it wasn't. He left her there crying while he dressed to go out and feed her father's cattle.

In the afternoon she had the house picked up and a meal waiting. She watched while he ate, but they didn't talk. He asked if she wanted to go to the funeral, and she said no and that was all. When he was drinking his coffee, calm now, and so tired his chest ached, he started thinking about Clara. He wondered if she'd known. Wouldn't have made any difference, he thought. Not after everything else.

Three days later, heading for the burial, he was alone and hunched against the wheel, driving through new snow that softly drifted across the highway. His fingers were numb, the broken cracks in the rough calluses ingrained with black. A tire chain ticked a fender, but he kept going. He'd gone out at daylight to feed, a mandatory job that had to be done every day of winter, regardless of other obligations. The rust-streaked Chevrolet swayed on the rutted ice beneath the snow. The steady and lumbering gait of the team he fed with, two massive frost-coated Belgian geldings, the creaking oceanic motion of the hay wagon, was still with him, more real than this.

The Derrick County cemetery was just below the road, almost five miles short of town. They were going to bury Art in the area reserved for charity burials, away from the lanes of Lombardy poplars and old-time lilacs. By dark the grave would be covered with snow. Ben parked and got out, and went over to look down in the hole. Far away in town, the bells of the Catholic church were faintly tolling. Ben stood a moment, then started back toward the car. He sat in the front seat with his hands cupped in his crotch, warming them. After a time, he backed slowly out of the graveyard.

Davanero was on the east side of the valley, scattered houses hung with ice, windows sealed against wind by tacked-on plastic sheeting. The still smoke of house fires rose straight up. Ben drove between lots heaped with snow-covered junk, past shacks with open, hanging doors where drifters lived in summer, into the center of town. The stores were open and a few people moved toward the coffee shops. He felt cut away from everything, as if this were an island in the center of winter.

The OPEN sign hung in the front window of The Tarpaper

Shack. Ben wondered if Clara was tending bar and if she intended to go to the funeral. He parked and walked slowly through the snow to the door. The church bells were louder, close and direct now. Inside, the tavern was dark and barnlike, empty except for Clara, who was washing glasses in a metal sink. Ben went to the far end, where Art always sat, and eased onto a stool. "I'd take a shot," he said. "A double. Take one yourself."

"I'm closing up," she said. "So there's no use hanging around." She stayed at the sink and continued to wash the glasses.

"You going to the funeral?" Ben said.

"I'm closing up." Her hands were still in the water. "I guess you need a drink," she said. "Go lock the door."

She was sitting in one of the booths when he got back. "You ain't going to the funeral?" he asked again.

"What good is that?"

"I guess you feel pretty bad."

"I guess." She drank quietly. "I would have took anything off him. Any damned thing. And that stupid bitch kills him. I would have given anything for his kid."

Ben finished his whiskey, and Clara took his glass and went for some more. "To hell with their goddamned funeral," he said.

Clara played some music on the juke box, slow country stuff; and they danced staggering against the stools and the shuffleboard table, holding each other. She pushed him away after a few songs. "If you ain't one hell of a dancer," she said. "Art was a pretty dancer." She sat down in the booth and put an arm on the table and then lay her head alongside it, facing the wall. "Goddamn," she said. "I could cry. I ain't cried since I was a little girl," she said. "Not since then. Not since I was a little girl."

Ben wandered around the barroom, carrying his drink. He called his wife on the telephone. "You bet your sweet ass I'm drunk," he shouted when she answered, then hung up.

"Ain't you some hero," Clara said. She drank what whiskey was left in her glass. "You're nothing," she said. "Absolutely nothing."

Outside, the bells had stopped. Nothing. That was what he felt like. Nothing. Like his hands were without strength to steer the car. He sat awhile in the front seat, then drove to the jail, a gray brick building with heavy wire mesh over the windows. The deputy, a small bald man in a gray uniform, sat behind a desk in the center of the main room, coffee cup beside him. He smiled when he saw Ben, but he didn't say anything.

"How's chances of seeing that girl?" Ben asked. He didn't know why he'd come. It was just some idea that because she'd hated Art enough to kill him, because of that, maybe she understood and could tell him, Ben, why he wasn't nothing. He knew, even while he spoke, that it was a stupid, drunk idea.

"Okay," the deputy said, after a minute. "Come on. I guess you got a right."

They went through two locked doors, back into a large cinder-block room without any windows. Light came from a long fluorescent tube overhead. Two cells were separated by steel bars six inches apart. The room was warm. The girl was sitting on a cot in the left-hand cell, legs crossed, with red hair straight down over her shoulders and wearing a wrinkled blue smock without pockets. She was looking at her hands, which were folded in her lap. "What now?" she said when she looked up. Her voice was surprisingly loud.

"Ben wanted to see you," the deputy said.

"Like a zoo, ain't it." The girl grinned and raised and lowered her shoulders.

"And you're not one bit sorry?" Ben said. "Just a little bit sorry for what you did?"

"Not one bit," the girl said. "I've had plenty of time to think about that. I'm not. I'm happy. I feel good."

"He wasn't no bad man," Ben said. "Not really. He never

really was."

"He sure as hell wasn't Winston Churchill. He never even *tried* to make me happy." She put her hands in her lap.

"I don't see it," Ben said. "No way I can see you're right. He wasn't that bad."

"The thing I liked about him," she said, "was that he was old enough. He was like you. He was old enough to do anything. He could have been nice if he'd wanted."

The deputy laughed.

"I felt so bad before," the girl said, "killing him was easy. The only thing I feel bad about is that I never got down into him and made him crawl around. That's the only thing. I'm sorry about that, but that's all."

"He didn't owe you nothing," Ben said.

The girl looked at the deputy. "Make him leave," she said.

Ben drove slowly home in the falling snow. He could only see blurred outlines of the trees on either side of the lane that led to his house. He parked the car, kicked the snow from his boots, and went inside the house. Marie was in the bedroom, sleeping. The dim room was gray and cold, the bed a rumpled island. Marie was on her back, her stomach a mound beneath the blankets. Her mouth gaped a little.

After he got out of his clothes, Ben sat on the edge of the bed. Marie sighed in her sleep and moved a little, but she didn't waken. Ben reached to touch her shoulder and then stopped. Her eyelids flickered open. "Come on," she said. "Get under the covers."

"In a minute," Ben said. He went back out to the kitchen and smoked a cigarette. Then he went back into the bedroom and crawled in beside her and put his hand on her belly, hoping to feel the baby move. He remembered a warm, shirt-sleeve day in February, working with Art, hurrying while they fed a final load of bales to the cattle that trailed behind, eager to get to town, noon sun glaring off wind-glazed fields of snow.

Flight

HEADING WEST out of Boise and looking down from a small aircraft, a twin-engine Cessna at six or seven thousand feet, the croplands near Caldwell are divided into perfectly rectangular fields; fenced, leveled, sectioned by irrigation ditches. In summer the atmosphere is dusty blue, cloudless, and the fields are variegated shades of green; alfalfa, feed corn, barley, rows of sugar beets, potatoes; crops which are rotated, fertilized, irrigated.

Further west the landscape changes and dries, turns brownish. Across the Snake River and the Malheur, past Ontario and Vale, the monotony of recurring lava-shelf rims and brushy sand hills becomes oppressive. The great shale-faced, two- and three-thousand-foot geologic fault ridges rise abruptly and then fall gradually away, sloping toward the west and the Pacific Ocean.

Beneath the steep eastern fall of those ridges lie occasional marshy and land-locked valleys where the headquarters buildings of cattle ranches sit on knolls beside the creeks. Water birds nest and lead their young into spring sloughs already green with algae.

The aircraft reaches the scattered beginnings of jack-pine and lodgepole just short of the Cascade peaks and the water-filled crater of Mount Mazama, banks and turns back. It passes over Burns and Lakeview, Paisley, Plush, Adel, Frenchglen in the Donner and Blitzen Valley; circles the three-story chimney preserved from the fire which destroyed Peter French's white frame ranch house. (French drove fifteen hundred head of cattle from Willows in the Sacramento Valley in

1872 when this country was unpopulated by white men except for John Devine at Whitehorse.) The aircraft passes the blackish volcanic cone of Iron Mountain and the valley of the Double O Ranch that belonged to Bill Hanley; continues east over Roaring Spring and Steen's Mountain, Fish Lake and Kiger Gorge, over the Miller and Lux country of the Alvord desert, where Chinamen dug Borax which was hauled south to Winnemucca in ore wagons drawn by oxen; flies over the weathervane on the horse barn at Whitehorse where Old Man Devine raced his thoroughbreds on a circular track in the 1880s; and then turns back over the Donner and Blitzen Valley, where Peter French's death by homesteader's rifle in 1897 marked the end of the free world — at least as freedom was understood then, in eastern Oregon, as open land and country to run.

[OWNING IT ALL]

"Give some people the world," the old man said, "and they wouldn't use it as nothing more than a place to read books." Toward the end he got so he'd say things like that, stand there in his only suit and spit something in his harsh voice and then turn away and that was that.

Maybe it was a result of being alone so much. Anyway, Old Man Fuller was like those others – Peter French and Devine and the men who'd opened the country; like Bill Brown who once owned 4,000 horses over around Wagontire. Those men got stubborn and set as they grew old and Fuller was like them, surely no exception.

He'd come horseback from somewhere east of the Owyhee River as a young man, leaving behind no family he ever spoke of, except to say he'd been raised poor, as if he'd sprung from the desert somewhere south of Mountain Home. Actually, in a year and a half of traveling he'd come all the way from the gumbo country around Belle Fourche in South Dakota. Just before 1900 he settled into the Willowtrail Valley, and by the end of the Depression he owned all the flat. What got him the property, he said, was work.

Peat ground cut by sloughs, six or seven miles wide, varying as the eastern sand hills encroached on the meadows, the Willowtrail ran north and south nearly fifteen miles. "No finer property," the old man said, sitting in the evening on his veranda, talking to his grandson, his namesake, another Carl Fuller. "High country in the heat of the season and perfect irrigation. Never a dry year."

Moths batted the screens and summer evening began beyond the light fading on the lawn grass. "I went down to Ryolite," the old man said. "Come back with seven hundred dollars from working a season in the silver mines and bought a hundred and sixty-four acres from a man named Sylvan Dixon. I come too late for free land and I was out of money."

It wasn't until the summer he died, in 1950, that his grandson learned what happened next. "I went over and stole fifty-three cows from the Indians at Summit Lake," the old man said. "All of them going to calve. That was 1897. By then the free days was over. There wasn't no Christmas presents." Carl Fuller watched his grandfather stand and walk stiff-legged toward the door opening into the living room. "That's one thing you'll learn," the old man said, "that's worth knowing."

One way or another, the old man bought his neighbors out, sometimes, in a hard winter, getting a half section for only a wagonload of groceries. Mostly the idea began during the First World War. By then his wife was dead and he was raising his only son, Carl's father, with a housekeeper, his days centering into work, summer on the desert and winters feeding cattle. It started with the idea there wasn't enough to do. Men were dying in France and he was wasting out his afternoons, working a little on hay equipment and then wandering up to sit by a fire in the living room of the house he'd built in 1906.

It seemed he should have enough work to fill his days, work to tire him and send him to sleep early. More land would mean more work, and that's what he wanted. In the beginning it was that simple. So he began to think of ways to get more land, and after awhile the land became more important than the work.

It came quickly and easily during the hard times of the early Twenties. By 1927 he owned half the valley and owed over a hundred thousand dollars and then in the summer of 1929 he sold enough acreage to pay off his debts with cheap dollars, that one lucky deal sending him into the Depression with no cash but at the same time, unencumbered. By the middle thirties he was able to mortgage the land for cheap government loans and by 1940 he owned all but 900 acres of the valley floor. By the end of the war he owned it all, most of it bought cheap in the midst of failure.

So in 1950, ready to die, he could sit on the veranda and look over the valley where the roads were his own, the water was his, everything, the second largest ranch in Panack County and the sixth or seventh largest in southeastern Oregon. "The best," he'd say. "Best this side of the Rockies." Not the biggest but the best, that was the idea. And in the idea somewhere was the thought that it was best because it was all together, one piece, because he owned it – he owned the whole valley.

[THE NIGHT OF JUNE 17, 1966]

Carl Fuller was almost asleep, when he began to imagine things. The woman who, he knew, had been his grandmother, stood breathing heavily on the steps, just in front of the screen door. Clumps of lilac on either side of the door were beginning to bloom and the blooms were dark, purple-black.

Carl Fuller was surprised at her youth. The woman was surely less than thirty and resembled his daughter, who was fourteen. How could this be? The woman seemed frightened or excited and continued staring and gasping soundlessly – as if not enough air could reach her.

Carl Fuller opened his eyes and raised up on his arm. Then he knew where the woman had been staring at – at the 30-30 rifle in the arms of his grandfather on Memorial Day, 1934.

His grandfather had just killed Tom Brotherton with the old rifle which was now used at the slaughterhouse to kill cows.

Carl Fuller lit a cigarette and remembered that single rapping sound. A hostile sound, unlike any shot heard since, singular and identifiable. Carl was four years old then and looking down at the face of Tom Brotherton, the flesh over those cheeks old and creased and granular, ingrained, as were all the desert faces, with a wind-driven grimace, coarsened by age. A food-stained gray silk neckerchief was tied under the stiff beard which waggled thick with grease and dust. The beard was pale beneath, as if its underside had never before this death been exposed.

While Carl stared, the small entry hole beneath the chin went on pumping blood onto the ground, into the dust, staining the gray silk bandana and the ragged collar of Tom Brotherton's heavy wool black-and-white check shirt. And all the time Carl was aware of his grandmother behind him on the steps and yet knew she could not be. She had died in 1911, before she was thirty, and this killing had happened in 1934, years after. She died on the 14th of May, 1911.

1911 was a good year, three-foot snow in the lower meadows of the mountains and heavy drifts through the timber, and a slow spring thaw. The irrigation water lasted until August. The old man had talked to Carl of 1911 and the death of his wife, of the injustice of that fine spring, the still and tranquil early days of that May, days that seemed endless.

Carl had listened and imagined the early heat of May, false summer before the cold rainstorms of June; late July in the heat and a heavy work-team sweating and moving in their harness and a slow, creaking buckrake pushing hay across a yellowing stubblefield toward a stackyard; drinking water in the dusty, light-streaked shade beneath the sloping planks of the ten-foot-high beaverslide the stacking crew had used even then to lift the hay while they piled it for winter, the metallic taste of water cold in a tin cup.

And his grandfather, alone, without the woman he had taken for himself with the idea she would be with him until his own death, who had borne him one son and then died; and he mourned over that long-ago summer of 1911 and getting the work done while reconstructing the reasons for doing it.

Carl could see the five-year-old who was his father crying and pulling at her left sleeve, trying to wake her. She died while hanging the wash on lines back of the house, white sheets and flour-sack pillow cases scrubbed on a rippling metal board. She fell down and lay quietly, as if sleeping, in the loose spring dust beneath those lines while a slight breeze came down the creek canyon and moved the items on the line. A corner of the sheet she was pinning there trailed a light, curving track in the dust; her wicker basket remained nearly full.

She lay in those old clothes, a yellow apron tied around her and the loose sleeves of a man's shirt pushed above her elbows, the tiny boy who was his father crouching over her. The scene flickered rapidly, passing to afternoon, past the man in ragged black clothing, his grandfather, returning at last from irrigating, shovel thrown against the fence, the tall pie-faced gelding he was riding, the quickening scenes of man, boy, death – for whatever mysterious reasons – on a cloudless morning in the middle of May.

Watching the child who was his father and the man who was his grandfather while they bent over the figure of the grandmother who died behind the house she had moved into after marrying his grandfather the fall of 1907, seeing that woman dead, watching that, Carl Fuller got up out of bed. In front of the house lay Tom Brotherton, the man killed by his grandfather in a dispute over a red and white yearling steer. He lay in sun among weeds, mostly Russian thistle, the shadow of cottonwood leaves flickering over the lower part of his body while the sun remained always at two o'clock on Memorial Day afternoon, while somehow that long-dead grandmother stood on the porch steps and looked and was frightened until at last

Carl stepped out onto the porch and looked around and shook his head.

[BROKEN FILM]

In Greece they called it *Ekphrasis*, the still movement. The old man's burial in 1950 was a series of tableaux which formed summations of the past and projections toward the future, contained the past and implied the future, still movements under late August sun. Like a yellowing film, occasionally stopped for repairs, the glaring light making it seem the incandescent bulb behind everything would soon burn through, as if it all would flare in flaming color on the screen, erupt and be gone.

Shortly after three in the afternoon, followed by almost thirty other automobiles, all with headlights glowing yellow through the dust, the Chrysler hearse from Alexander's Funeral Home eased down the gravel roadways between small, untended graveyard plots, under sixty-year-old homesteaders' apple trees and between rows of slowly maturing evergreen, and parked alongside the lilac near the open hole. Flowers were already in place, horseshoe wreaths tied with velvet ribbons, vases of second-rate drugstore flowers rushed from the small Episcopal Church on the north side of town. The men in the hearse sat quietly, sweating, while the other automobiles circled, waited, parked.

Eight pallbearers, two of them very old, of his generation; the others all somewhere between fifty-five and seventy, the younger men big and strong, faces burned and lined by lives spent working out of doors. The preacher, thin and balding, maybe thirty-five, out of place, an outsider and disregardable, finished his talk. Women were quiet in veils and flowered hats. Then one of the pallbearers coughed, a man named Jacobson. As he gestured at wiping his mouth the moment ended, his white handkerchief seeming a signal; and people began turning away, moving slowly, men in suits, dusty shoes, wives with their babies, children following, old brown and withered hands, veined and liver-spotted, resting lightly on arms enclosed in sleeves that had grown too large.

The glare grew more intense, covering sounds, and in their slow movements, as they talked and pressed hands and smiled secretly they seemed to express indifference for death. This burial was not their own; a hummingbird paused in the lilacs; theirs would never come.

The Soap Bear

A NEW WORLD every morning. Every night, Banta thought, every time the sun turns sideways. *Rock of ages, near to thee,* crooning through the static from the Hallicrafter radio, voices in rising harmony while the postcard scenes of his life hung on another slope, his bluebird mornings slipped away, back into the white noise that scratched with the music.

So now Grace was dead, and Danzig was dead, and they all were dead. Someone would have to clean up the mess. But not me, Banta thought. Banta stood with his hands on the cold enamel rim of the kitchen sink, studying the elongated shadows of light cast out from the windows. They lay soft as reflections of a summer moon on the new snow.

Sparks from the exhaust of the pumping, diesel-fueled electric generator fanned away into the twilight like mid-winter fireflies. Banta dug a yellow stocking cap from the pocket of his sheepskin coat, and orange-tinted skier's goggles, and went out into the cold where he tightened the cinch around the belly of his black gelding. Then he climbed up into the saddle and rode away.

How to stay alive in the snowy woods – old lessons. *Avoid panic. Think of taking hostages.* Virgil Banta rode an unplowed lane between bare-limbed cottonwoods and across the echoing bridge above Marshall Creek, down toward the Clark Fork of the Columbia and the highway. The snow fell steadily, as it had since the third day after Christmas, large fragile flakes dropping through the windless cold.

Do not be afraid of telling lies. Remember that, remember this, remember every detail, every step of this way. In the snowy woods. Instructions from Danzig. But Danzig was dead.

Just down the hill from the fence where Danzig lay frozen half-under the snow, Virgil Banta climbed from the gelding. Banta thought of Danzig frozen, those strong white fingers stiff enough to break clean off like sticks if you hit them with a hammer. Danzig had been plowing the road in from the highway when he died. When Banta shot him. The angle-bladed cable-drum old D7 Caterpillar was a dark shadow up in the jack pine where it stalled after Danzig fell off the seat, dead. Banta opened his pants and stood pissing, his blood-stiff yellow buckskin gloves tucked under one arm. When he finished, standing over the steaming hole in the snow, he picked for a moment at the frozen clotted blood with a thumbnail, tossed the gloves into a thicket of buckbrush below the road, and climbed on the gelding once more, settling into the skiff of snow already feathering on the seat of his high-forked saddle.

When Virgil Banta reached the highway along the river, and night settled into the steep-walled canyon, two does and a forked-horn buck came to lick at the salty yellow stain where he had pissed. In the brushy thicket a porcupine began to gnaw at the bloody gloves.

Another slope of his life. The year Virgil was ten and his sister Grace was eight, that summer their friend Skinny Burton died of drowning, his sharp-ribbed body white and limp in red bathing trunks on the grass between two willow tree stumps. A Sunday afternoon, and their father crouched over Skinny, pumping at his chest, while a thin dribble of water ran from Skinny's nose, but Skinny was dead.

Grace stayed to watch. Virgil ran and hid in the cool meathouse where blocks of creek-ice survived the summer under wet sawdust. Virgil chipped slivers off the ice and sucked them. The dim interior of that insulated building was very quiet. His only visitor was a calico mouse-hunting cat.

That night on the screened-in veranda overlooking the valley of the Bitterroot River, he asked his mother if dead people cry. "No," his mother said, her arm heavy around his shoulder, "your grandmother didn't cry when she was dying."

Virgil could remember the endless raspy voice of his grandmother singing unintelligible wheezing verses of some song from her childhood in the back bedroom before she died. Lights from the other ranches out in the shadowland of meadow and willow where Virgil was a child, those lights flickered as they shone through the screen around the porch. Virgil could make them flicker by moving his head. His father came home from the funeral parlor in Hamilton, where Skinny Burton was being drained of creekwater and his blood, and dressed and rouged to look the way he looked three days later in an open coffin. The dull red GMC pickup rattled over the cattle-guard by the barn and stopped just short of the porch, nosing into the light. His father looked old and tired as he stood in the kitchen sipping coffee and smelling of whiskey.

"How could he cry?" Grace said later, sitting up on her bed in their attic bedroom where frost would form on the rafters in wintertime. She had long braids, and her face was scrubbed and gleaming under the single bulb dangling from the ridgepole. "He was under the water."

Under the water, Banta thought.

Virgil lay quiet that night after Grace was asleep and listened to her breathe. He wondered what it would be like dying under the water, looking up to the light. And now Grace was dead, and she *had* cried – there had been tears on her face when she died. Grace was dead, and Danzig was dead, and up there in the house they were all dead, and he'd killed them.

The storms came in from the Pacific, over the Cascades and the flatland wheatfields of eastern Washington. All his life Shirley Holland had watched them come over the Bitterroot Mountains to play out and dump themselves in Montana, snow falling in the soft wind that blew flakes down the streets like dust.

It was like the coming and going of seawater. Like the drift of tide.

In the kitchen, under the sink with the bottles of bleach and ammonia, there was an unopened bottle of Sunnybrook. Shirley Holland bought Sunnybrook because he liked the name. Carefully he cut the plastic seal with the tip of his knife and poured a couple of inches into a water glass, the whiskey glowing amber like fishing water in the late days of fall. *A new world every morning.* He had been a young man then, the third year he was Sheriff, when he hired a traveling sign painter to print those words in three-foot-high black letters across the outside wall of his cinder-block jailhouse. It was something he learned from his father. The old man had been talking about drunks locked in the tank to sober up overnight, and about himself when he got old and couldn't remember the seasons. In old age his father had lived by himself, and said he sometimes woke in the morning and looked out expecting to see snow and found himself surprised by blossoming lilac. You would think a man would know, his father said, just by the light. His voice trailed off, and he stared at the wall as if amazed to discover such a fool in himself. The old man hadn't sympathy for drunks, even when he was drinking himself. Shirley Holland thought of those words every time he started at the whiskey. *A new world every morning.* Faded words lettered on the side of his jailhouse like a motto for his life.

Shirley Holland was at his kitchen table, sipping his second glass of whiskey, when someone pounded at the living room door. "Doris," he said, "tell them to go across the street and see Billy."

But after she mumbled to whoever it was, Doris came scuffing down the hallway toward him in her buckskin slippers. "Holland," she said, "you better come out here."

"Tell them I'm not in business," Shirley Holland said.

Doris chewed at her upper lip, staring at her reflection in the dark window over the sink. "The thing is," she said, "he looks exactly like you." She glanced toward Holland, one of her

quick old-time looks, part grin, that took him back to the barroom years when they courted and ran together before they
were married. Maybe this was another shot at what she had
taken to talking about as her joking. Just this last year she had
gone distant and strange on him. After sixteen years, this
woman with her rimless schoolteacher eyeglasses and her
blonde hair going thin and gray now, had gone away from
him. On Christmas day, spooning oyster dressing out of their
turkey, just the two of them because there hadn't been any
children – she didn't want children growing up in a sheriff's
house was her excuse for having her tubes tied off – she started
talking about a song she heard on the radio, a song called
"Satan's Jewel Crown." Doris said it made her think about
those people out there who were courting the devil by cutting
the tongues and privates out of dead cows and leaving the rest.
She said the song made her sad because no one ever offered to
ruin her life, and she said she was thinking about spending the
spring in San Francisco.

"Even Coit Tower," she said, "I never even been to Coit
Tower. I would have gone with a woman even. If she'd asked
me." Holland hadn't answered, just took himself a helping of
string beans and let it drop. That night, looking up from a
fancy picture book about the lives of French kings, she said it
was a joke. "That part about a woman in San Francisco, anyway," she said, "that was a joke." "Funny as hell," Shirley
Holland said, and she looked at him and shook her head.

Now, someone waiting at the front door, she was shaking
her head again, like Holland was responsible for terrible sadness everywhere, like she could cry.

"Looks the spitting image of you," she said.

"Only maybe," she said, and out of her sadness she grinned,
"he might be left-handed."

The kid didn't look anything like him, just some big-shoul-
dered kid, maybe twenty years old, wearing a yellow knit skier's cap, with ice and snow in his long hair and beard, but a
working kid from the looks of his hands. But then maybe Doris

wasn't joking. The kid looked like the son of somebody Holland had known.

"There is trouble," the kid said in a flat voice, as though it was nothing of much consequence. "Out to that Danzig house up there on Marshall Creek."

"There ain't no Danzig house," Shirley Holland said, "you mean the Frantz place."

"The place that Danzig fellow leased," the kid said.

"There sure as hell is something wrong out there," Shirley Holland said. "You one of them?"

"My sister was Grace. My name is Virgil Banta. You knew my father. He was Mac Banta."

The kid pulled off his yellow stocking cap. His eyes were dark points in the dim entryway light. "There has been a crowd of people killed," he said.

"My sister," he said, "they killed Grace." Shirley Holland wondered what to do with this, as he watched the kid's eyes fill with tears. It was like watching an animal begin to weep.

The inside of the four-wheel-drive Chevrolet pickup cab was warm enough. The wipers were swiping and the heater was blowing hot air out the defroster vents and onto his hands, and the air smelled of tobacco and sweaty clothing. But every twenty or so minutes Shirley Holland would have to stop and let the deputy, Billy Kumar, get out and break the ice off the wipers, and then Holland would feel the brittle midnight cold. Billy would get back inside with snow on his red and black timber-cruiser jacket and everything would stink a little worse of damp wool, like drowned sheep.

"It's the bombs," Billy Kumar said, talking about the weather, "every time they set off another of them nuclear bombs."

Shirley Holland chewed at a matchstick. His shoulders ached. The ruts in the road were frozen hard, and the pickup rocked and churned, the steering wheel bucking in his hands. Almost half a lifetime of herding drunks, watching while some mechanic with a cutting torch released the body of another drunk from the crushed interior of an old car, or maybe a woman shotgunned while she was sleeping in bed. One whiskey-stinking wreck or bedroom after another, and then a long afternoon in the office, typing up reports. And now this deputy, Billy Kumar, dumber than rocks and talking about bombs.

"Never been the same," Billy Kumar said gesturing quickly with the left hand where he wore a heavy silver ring with a setting of polished green opal. Billy held his buff-colored Stetson between his knees and fingered endlessly at the band, turning the hat counterclockwise as he did.

"Where did you get that ring?" Shirley Holland asked.

"Last year in Las Vegas."

"Makes you look like a queer."

Billy Kumar didn't answer. Maybe it *was* the bombs, Holland mused. Snow before Thanksgiving, and then right before Christmas, days of spring-like thaw and flooding, bridges washing out, and now this week of blizzard. At least they were not out here on horseback, freezing their asses. They were only a little more than a mile from the house. In the old days the place had been run as a hunting camp. This was before Amos Frantz died and his property sold. Hunting camp and part-time whorehouse. Since then there hadn't been any sort of hunting camp. In the old days there weren't any of these rich people playing at make-believe, dressing up in Indian costumes and riding snowmobiles. "There's gamblers in Las Vegas wearing rings like this," Billy Kumar said, "and nobody better call them queers."

They were right at the fence the kid had talked about, just down from where that D7 Cat was stalled up on the hillside in the jack pines. The canyon sloped up out of the headlights on that side, and to the right was the darkness that was the wash of Marshall Creek. From here the road wouldn't be even half plowed. "Billy," Holland said, "you take a rest. You wait for me right here."

After tying one of Doris's old nylon stockings over his ears like a headband and pulling his stockman's hat down, Holland stepped out into fluffy new snow that was knee-deep over the old frozen crust, and started climbing toward the dark shadow of that D7 Caterpillar. The hillside was so steep it looked as if the machine might, if somebody only touched it, rock and turn slowly and come thundering down. But the question was: what the hell was it doing there?

Holland was resting with his hands on his knees, out of wind, head down and dizzy, and thought maybe it was something he imagined when he heard Billy Kumar shout. Then another shout, muffled and echoing, and frightened, and he knew it was Billy. The deputy had turned over the frozen, snowy body of a dead man. "You didn't see him, did you?" Billy said. "There was an arm sticking up. I saw it plain as hell. God Almighty."

The damned fool, Shirley Holland thought. Now we've got this, and he's got himself scared shitless. Billy had jerked on the arm and found he had hold of a frozen hand, and he'd fallen backward. He stood there covered with snow and looking frightened enough to cry. Shirley Holland knelt beside the body and brushed the snow from the face.

"One of them kids," he said, but it wasn't a kid at all. He brushed more snow from the face. This was Danzig, a fifty-year-old man, features distorted in the lights from the pickup reflecting off the snow, just a thin face and long hair iced into thick brittle strands. Shirley Holland kept brushing away the snow and then stopped. This dead man, whose features he was polishing like stone, had been shot, the bullet entering in a neat small high-velocity hole just in front of and above the right ear and passing out through the back of the neck, leaving a jagged frozen wound the size of a teacup. The hard flesh was rough as wood to the touch, the mouth half-closed on a twisted upper plate, and the eyes turned up, open and blank, frosted white.

There was nothing to say. Billy Kumar made a move like he was going to run, but held his ground. "Get hold of his feet," Holland said. "I'll take the head."

"You think so," Billy Kumar said, "you think we ought to

move him right away?"

"Yeah," Shirley Holland said, "we ought to move him."

The body was frozen sprawled, arms and legs spread like a starfish. Holland dropped his end twice before they reached the pickup. His chest ached, and his hands didn't have any feeling. "You ain't even thirty years old," Shirley said, "so don't be looking at me. You just lift him over the tailgate, else we are going to be here all night."

With his eyes closed, Billy got hold of the body, arms around the dead man's waist. The snow-covered steel flooring of the pickup bed echoed dully when they dropped the frozen body inside. They warmed themselves in the pickup cab, and Billy turned the radio to country music. Roger Miller singing, *Trailer for sale or rent*. Shirley wanted to laugh. How long since he had heard that song? There had been a night drinking and dancing with whatever women were around when they had played that song over and over. He never noticed when songs went off the jukebox. Back around 1965, at least that far back. "If I'm going to concentrate," Holland said, "you are going to shut that off."

Why concentrate? The thing to do was go back for help. But that didn't feel right. The kid was there with Doris. "You don't leave town," he had told the kid. "He can stay here," Doris said. "I'll fix some bacon and some eggs. Just like home." The kid had wiped the tears out of his eyes and smiled at her.

"There is a ghost up here," Shirley Holland said to Billy Kumar. The pickup was plowing two or so feet of dry snow, but not lurching in the ruts the way it had. "There's a ghost of a dead Chinaman."

When he was eleven or twelve, the first of the hunting campouts his father had trusted him with, the men had told him a story about a Chinese camp cook who died and had been buried in the foundation of the house. "We rocked him up under the south corner," his father said, "to keep the coyotes away. The next spring he was dried up and there was no smell at all."

"Under there," his father said, showing him the rock pile against the southeast corner of the house. "His bones are under there yet if his people ain't come for him. Them people believe in things like that, ghosts coming for your bones."

Billy Kumar was fingering his hatband again. "There ain't no ghosts," Shirley Holland said, "no more than there are ghosts of cows."

In an upstairs bedroom Amos Frantz kept a whore from Butte whose name was Annie. She stayed most of one hunting season, and her feet had been caked with dirt as she cried and waved all the way across the bridge when Amos put her gear into his pickup and hauled her down the canyon and back to the Bluebird House in Butte. Flakes of snow lifted in the headlights like floating goose down. No ghosts at all.

One drunken night Holland had pissed into the fireplace, onto the burning cedar coals, up there in that house. Holland had been sleeping in the living room, and the snapping coals had kept him awake, and he had been trying to put them out while listening to the mumbled cursing of the other men bedded in the room. The stink of that scorching urine was with him now. The sandstone mantel over the fireplace had been darkened by soot over the years, and the next morning they had all carved their initials into the soft rock. Shirley Holland had carved an S H inside a heart.

Out in the clouding snow the house hovered like some lighted craft coming toward them, the glow diffusing into lapping auras in the falling snow, silt stippling the darkness. Shirley Holland refused to take the pickup across the bridge above Marshall Creek. "We'll walk it," he said. "Slide a wheel off that thing, and there you'll be."

Billy Kumar reached to lift the sawed-off 12-gauge shotgun from the rack behind the pickup seat. "You ain't going to need that," Shirley Holland said. "There ain't going to be anybody up there. The kid said there was nobody alive in there, and if there is they will shoot us while we're walking."

"Or be glad to see us," Holland said, reaching under the pickup seat for his bottle of Sunnybrook. "There's some of them people would be glad to see anybody."

Doris Holland was playing religious music from a Christmas album of four long-playing records, the only church music in the house. The *Messiah*. The long-haired boy, his name was Virgil Banta, wanted to hear something good for the soul. That was what he said, good for the soul. He was sitting cross-legged on the floor beside the record player, wearing an old flannel shirt of Holland's that almost fit. Just a little short in the sleeves. Doris had given him the shirt when he came out of the shower. She knocked at the door of the steamy bathroom to tell him the omelet was ready, with warmed-over lima beans and remnants of ham hocks on the side, and he had come out with no shirt on, rubbing his long hair with a towel, and his chest at least as furry as Holland's. She turned away and got him the washed-out shirt from Holland's chest of drawers.

Poor child with his sister dead. Doris had a brother, who was dead. Doris could still see her brother's rouged face turned up at the whitewashed rafters of the Methodist Church in Elk River, Idaho. All the people who had been there she hadn't seen for a long time – Dora and Slipper Count, small as wrinkled children in their seventies, hands shaking because they lived every day but Sunday on wine; and Marly Prester and his new wife; and the others, old man Duncan Avery and all those children.

The music stopped and the boy went on staring at his bare feet. Doris got up to turn the records and he stopped her. "That's not the music," he said.

"How come you want me to look like him?" the boy said.

"I don't want you to, you just do."

"That's your idea," he said.

His eyes were gray, the same as Holland's. "You fit his shirt," Doris said.

"Well, that about gets it," he said. "That's about all of his I would fit." He looked up and smiled slowly, like he had forgotten his sister was dead.

"How do you know that?" she said.

"Your feet get cold," he said, "you put on your hat. That's the rule. Your head is like a refrigerator, you have to turn it off to get your fingers and toes warm. So you put on your hat.

"That's rule number eleven," he said. "Danzig taught me that rule." He got up and went into the hallway where his yellow stocking cap was stuffed into the pocket of his sheepskin coat. He pulled the cap down over his wet hair. "Now," he said, "I don't feel no pain, because my head is covered.

"You got to do lots of things this way," he said, "with your head turned off. Danzig taught me all that. And how to stay alive. The boy laughed, and pulled off the stocking cap. "But now Danzig is dead," he said.

"You aren't like Holland at all," Doris said. "You only look like Holland, that's all."

"You'll get used to it," Virgil Banta said, sitting down on the floor again, this time right in front of where she sat on the couch. "Don't you think so?" he said. "I got used to Danzig. For a long time I was used to Danzig. But now Danzig is dead, and after a while they'll get me."

"I guess that doesn't make any sense," Doris said, holding herself very quiet because he was touching her foot, easing the slipper off her right foot and starting his fingers working softly between her toes. No, there was nothing in him that was at all like Holland, she thought. Poor child with a dead sister. It was important to keep knowing he was a poor child with a dead sister, and nothing around him but this house.

2

SEVEN ORANGE BACKPACKS, fully loaded, right down to tightly rolled sleeping bags, were lined along the far wall. The orange contrasted vividly against the sea-green wallpaper, and splattered across the orange nylon there was a spray of dried blood. But it wasn't the blood that surprised Shirley Holland, it was the warmth of the house, propane heat and the neatness of everything but the bodies. *Blown away*, Shirley Holland thought, *milk in the pudding*. Words of a song he'd known as a child. What could they mean now? The walls had been torn out so the ground floor was one room, including the kitchen, and there was the hardware: seven sets of binoculars on a dark table against the wall beside the packboards, seven leather cases that must contain binoculars. And the automatic rifles, Holland recognized them from pictures, leaning one by one alongside the packboards. And above all that, a slogan painted high on the green wall: THE SEVEN DWARFS. Each end of the room was decorated with a huge black-and-white poster, one of Ché Guevara and one of Chairman Mao. And there was a television set silently playing. The picture on the television set was the only thing moving. Shirley Holland turned away. "You best go wait in the pickup," he said to Billy Kumar, who was behind him on the entry porch.

"What if there is somebody?" Billy Kumar said.

"There ain't going to be nobody, at least nobody that ought to get us excited." Which was the old secret, do not get excited, look around and make sense of things, count the holes and think of reasons why. "There is not going to be a damned soul around here, soon as you go outside and turn off that television set." Shirley Holland turned to find Billy Kumar's short-barreled Detective Special .38 automatic aimed dead into his back.

"Billy," Shirley Holland said, "you might shoot me, and then where would we be? You go sit on the front steps." He figured Billy might drive off if he got near the pickup. "You just put that gun away and take a rest," Shirley Holland said. "All this is my problem, and none of yours."

On the television screen here was the dim luminous blue of early morning, and snow on low hills patched with evergreen. From far off a dark figure proceeded toward the camera, then the picture cut and the figure was closer, then a series of quick

cuts until the man on snowshoes was close enough to recognize. It was the dead man, the man Shirley Holland recognized
as Danzig. Another thing to try and make sense of. Shirley
Holland shut off the television while Danzig grinned into the
camera and pulled off his stocking cap. The same sort of cap
the kid had been wearing. Maybe they all wore caps. Holland
touched the granular sandstone mantel above the ash-filled
fireplace. Some one of these children had scrubbed the years of
soot from the yellow stone that was rough as sandpaper under
his fingertips, but his initials were still there, S H inside a heart,
alongside the names and initials of the men who had been his
friends in those days.

Now that he was able to look at them, there were five of them
dead in this big room. It was hard to tell which were the boys
and which were girls, what with their long hair and the same
kind of clothes, workshirts and raggedy Levi's and wool socks,
no shoes or boots on any of them, five dead children on that
hardwood floor. Five was the right number. There was Danzig
dead in the pickup, and there was the kid in town with Doris.
That added up to seven. Seven backpacks and seven sets of
binoculars and seven automatic rifles and the sign on the wall:
THE SEVEN DWARFS. That made it perfect.

They must have sanded and varnished the floor because it
shone like it never had in the old days. The green wall was
tattooed with bullet holes in two long undulating rows, holes
that could only have been made by one of the automatic rifles
leaning against the green wall by the backpacks. The weapons
were Swedish BAR, M-37, and loaded. Shirley Holland lifted
one and was surprised at how heavy it was in his hands. As he
held the automatic rifle he imagined old television pictures of
vague jungles in Vietnam, and they changed with the weight
of that rifle in his hands; he could nearly taste the sour green of
the swampy tropics as he held the rifle waist high and turned,
imagining the heavy racketing sound the rifle would make, the
bullets fluttering around the room. If he went outside and fired

a couple of rounds into the propane tank the place would burn. "Billy," he called, and when he looked out the open door there was Billy with flakes of snow melting on his plaid jacket, still holding the .38 Detective Special.

"Billy," Holland said, "you put the safety on, and put that damned thing away. Make yourself a snowball or something. There is not going to be anybody here."

Then Holland turned away and did it, he touched the trigger and the rifle jumped in his hands, stronger and more forceful than he had imagined, the sound louder, battering and harsh inside that room, quicker than he had thought; and there was another short row of bullet holes in the green wall, Holland thought, *Billy, there's Billy out on the porch,* and he spun, ready to fall and roll if Billy should come in shooting and crazy, but only ended up standing there with the automatic rifle aimed at the open doorway.

Heading for the pickup, he thought, and he imagined Billy running down through the snow, toward the bridge. Should have got his keys away from him. "Billy," Holland said, "you all right?"

"Yeah." Billy stepped through the doorway. He was smiling, and the .38 was in his shoulder holster.

"What we're going to do," Shirley Holland said, surprised by the idea as he said it, "is stay the night, and see what is what around here." He waited for the insolence to slip out of Billy's eyes.

"There is food on the stove," Billy said. "They were cooking. Someone shut off the burners." Billy was shaking a pair of silver-mounted spurs with rowels big as cartwheel dollars, and the clinking sound was like someone slowly walking. "These spurs," Billy said, as if there was nothing to fear, "were on a nail out there. Whoever it was had to be horseback. There's no tracks otherwise."

Billy clinked the spurs again, his eyes almost vacantly intent, like the business of this night had seared over the soft place in his head that made him always afraid. Holland knew what it was, the overload from seeing too many bodies. Enough of that and the dead become different from you, no more important than broken chairs.

"Billy," Shirley Holland said, "we better have a drink. We better warm some of that stew and have a drink. What you do, you warm up whatever they were eating and I'll walk down to the pickup and get the bottle." His hands were shaking, and Holland knew he was not going to stay the night. What a crazy idea! The idea was have some hot food and a drink, and then leave. When he was outside, halfway down the lane toward the bridge, Holland realized he was still carrying the automatic rifle, and he laid it carefully in the snow, walked a few more feet, then went back and carried the rifle down to the bridge and dropped it off into the darkness where the small stream had cut away the drifted snow.

The stew was thick with chopped leeks. The girl dead on the floor just beyond the stove must have been a vegetarian, they must have all been vegetarians, because the only meat in the stew was bits of fish and shrimp and clams. With his belly filled, Shirley Holland was finally looking closely at one of the dead, the girl sprawled on the floor beyond the stove, near the long laboratory table where the elaborate Bausch and Lomb microscope, fitted out with camera attachments, sat like a huge gray metal mantis hibernating toward spring. Between the stove and the microscope a worn oriental rug hung like a tapestry from the ceiling, forming a room divider. The side nearest the stove was slick with grease. It was then, touching the rug, his belly warm with stew and whiskey hot in his throat, that Shirley Holland thought about vegetarians and knew he was wrong. Somebody had been frying meat.

The girl, when he brushed her long reddish hair back off her face, this one was clearly a girl, heavy-breasted in a white embroidered peasant's blouse, this girl's face was thin and almost foreign-looking. Even with that nose she must have been close to beautiful before she fell and bit halfway through her tongue.

"Maybe it's important," Holland said.

"What?" Billy Kumar was still carrying his spoon.

"That they turned off the stove." Whoever walked out of this alive had cared enough and been sensible enough to shut off the burners, which in turn meant not crazy. Or maybe it meant crazy enough, or else it meant nothing. Most likely it meant whoever it was had been used to taking care of things in this house. Which meant nothing again, because he knew the kid had been here. So maybe the kid had turned off the burners, even with his sister dead. Which one was the sister? Surely not this one, she couldn't be the sister, not with that nose.

"So maybe it's the kid," Billy Kumar said, "back there with Doris."

"Don't pay no attention about Doris," Shirley Holland said.

"That's Doris all right," Billy Kumar said.

"How's that?"

"Doris can do all right."

Shirley Holland grunted and turned on the light in the microscope and peered down through the eyepiece. The instrument was focused on what looked like a hair, thick and cellular in magnification against a glaring white background. Holland shut off the light. Looking through a thing like that was like driving through snow, it got you to seeing the wrong sides of complications where there was only this simple problem: what happened? And that was equally simple. Someone had sprayed these people with M-37 bullets, and the blood that had splattered everywhere in this room, the bullet holes in the green wall, that was what had been going on in here. It was time to go home. They ought to stop touching and moving things and send some fingerprint people to figure things out until the dark touch of a killer came clear.

"What I am going to do," Holland said, "is leave you here to stand guard. I am going back to town and let you look after things here for the night. Maybe whoever it is will come back, and you can get him."

Billy Kumar smiled like that was a good idea. "All right,"

Billy said, "you do that."

"Not really," Holland said. "Let's shut off the stove and close the door on this place."

"I mean it," Billy said. "It don't bother me a bit."

"It ought to," Holland said.

"Just so long as you see I ain't chickenshit," Billy said. "There's no way I am chickenshitting out on this. Just so you know that."

"I got that straight," Holland said. "You are not chickenshit. You are a hard man to frighten."

"That's good," Billy said. "There is nothing to worry about out here. He's back in town with Doris. Back there is where you got to start worrying."

It wasn't until then, watching Billy shut off the burners on the stove, the dying blue flicker of propane, that Holland knew which one was the sister. She was the one slumped at the foot of the stairway leading up to the second floor and the bedrooms. This was in some way her fault. Holland could see it, the kid standing near the doorway with the automatic rifle, the sister coming arrogantly down the stairs after the kid called her, his voice shrill and angry, some disdainful remark from the sister, dismissing his anger, and this touch of the finger, the hammering sound as the bullets traced their way back and forth across that green wall, and all of them dead. A quarrel from childhood finally resolved. But maybe it wasn't that way. Maybe Danzig had gone first, shot off that D7 in the late afternoon, as the kid rode in; maybe all this was planned.

There was no telling, but for sure no one but the kid could have stood there with the M-37 while they all went on about the business of their cookng. Only the kid could have swept the room with that M-37 like he was blowing it clean with a hose.

The girl at the bottom of the stairs had a plain country face and short dark hair, and Holland knew he was right. She was the sister. Holland stepped over her and climbed the stairs toward the darkness up there, and when he switched on the light in the room directly across from the head of the stairway, he knew he was even more right. It was a bedroom, there was no door, not even a curtain hanging in the doorway, no privacy, but it was a room where people slept. There was a double-bed mattress on the floor, covered with a fake-looking oriental rug that had been spattered with yellow paint, and a long table and a chair under the dark window in the far wall, but furnishings were not what was important. What mattered was the dead man. A small dark man, maybe a Puerto Rican or a Cuban or Malaysian, one of the fine-boned dark people from some other continent; he was curled in the far corner of the room, and had been chopped apart with short crossing sweeps of the M-37, literally cut up in the work of the night. His face was torn apart, and his intestines spilled and burst, blood and greenish fecal matter pooled together and drying on the flooring. The man had been naked except for a pair of avocado-green nylon bikini shorts. You poor lonesome little bastard, Holland thought, he got you fine, didn't he. Which will teach you to trust in white girls.

So this is the reason, Holland thought, the old reasons. Posters on the wall, and snowmobiles down in the barn where the teams of work-mares once steamed on winter mornings while they snuffled at their oats, automatic rifles and whatever these kids thought they were going to force toward perfection, and now there is this same old trouble. Danzig first; Danzig was older, and had money, and was just playing. Holland didn't blame the kid for getting Danzig first, making sure of that much.

The soap bear: the tiny precisely carved fangs.

The soap bear sat surrounded by whittled shards of the hard yellow laundry soap it had come from, alone on the table under the window except for the elaborately compartmented hardwood box of thin-bladed Exacto carving knives, chisels and tiny chrome-plated hammers, needles which might be used for etching. The girl had been starting herself a career in carving. Winter could lock you into seeing how you could be somebody else while you watched out a second-story window to where snowbirds were playing. Holland tested the blade of one of the Exacto knives against the back of his thumbnail. It was as factory sharp as any knife he had ever honed. Once in the lobby of the U.S. National Bank in Cody, Wyoming, waiting for a check to go through, Holland watched a man carve the head of an eagle from dark hardwood. That man had been using tools exactly like these. They looked like instruments that might belong to a dentist.

And how sure-handed she had been. Holland wondered if she had been at her carving just before she was called down the stairs to die. Holland could see it, the little dark man sleeping in his avocado-green undershorts, and the girl at her work, the call from downstairs, whatever tool she had been using placed neatly back into the compartmented box; and then the racketing of the automatic rifle when she reached the bottom of the stairway. Holland imagined the little dark man terrified and confused from his sleep as the killer came slowly up after him, the dark man cringing in the corner, and the unforgiving stare of the gunman. Not even then will you believe it, Holland thought, not until you are dead will you know it has happened.

Holland picked up the soap bear. The body was only roughed-in behind the shoulders, but the head was carved in great detail, the ears, the fangs, and the ruffled hump of a grizzly by someone who knew what she was doing. It was nice work. Those years ago they carved their names roughly in the sandstone mantle over the fireplace, and that roughness had worked out better than this fine touch. But maybe not: there was always the scorching odor of piss in that memory. Holland shook his head and went down the stairs, left the lights burning and headed out into the snow. "Which one," Billy said, "do you figure was the sister?"

"I figure they all was," Holland said, waiting on the porch, "I figure they was all his sister. We might as well get down the road."

"Not me," Billy said. "I'm staying here."

"You ain't hired to do what you want," Holland said.

"Fine," Billy said. "Then I quit. I'm staying here."

"I guess you are," Holland said. "You stay here. Never mind the quitting. You stay here and guard the evidence." Holland slipped the soap bear under his coat, where it would be out of the snow. The moisture might melt one of those fine touches. You stay here, he thought, and then you can figure on twenty years of not being upset by anything because you've seen it all now. It will do you good to stay.

When he reached the pickup, Holland shone his flashlight into Danzig's iced-over face. He brushed the snow away. Private television, he thought. You must have been one fancy asshole to gather all this trouble into one household. Billy had followed him down from the house. "There ain't no good in it," Billy said, "in staying here. In town is where the killer is."

3

FRILLED AND EMBROIDERED, the nylon robe swept the carpet silently as Doris Holland came barefoot into the living room. Sitting herself on the floor before the fireplace, she drew open the brass fire doors. Opening the leather-bound picture album, she quickly snapped three of the photographs from the holders fastening them to the page. She flicked each photo into the cold fireplace with a quick motion of her wrist. Then she reached in, and drew out the little pile of photographs, as if she must begin again, properly.

After switching on the small cut-glass chandelier in the room she took up the pictures again, this time examining each before dropping it into the fireplace. Occasionally, she would come across old photographs of Holland, a long-haired ragged boy squinting into the sun from the bed of a Ford v-8 truck, crouching with baby geese beside spring tules, pictures of old people she had never known, gone or dead before she ever saw Holland, a gray-haired woman, wearing a sagging flowered dress and a gambling-man sun visor, standing beside an ancient black automobile and scowling. These photos she set aside, intending them for Holland. Only when the pile for burning was bigger than she had imagined it could be – she never remembered posing for so many pictures – as she was heading down the hallway toward the kitchen for matches, did she think of how the fire would look, flame, and then a curling mound of cellulose that would resemble the final moments of a doll burning, the yellow feathery hair and the little clothes gone, the plastic body curling into the insides of itself. She pulled a hair from her head and struck a match and lighted the hair and watched it burn before she left the pictures piled there in the firebox and went back up the stairs to where the boy was sleeping. So many pictures of herself; Doris in a yellow dress, down by the river on a Sunday, her face soft and drunk and her bright lipstick in that fuzzy old-time World War II color, smeary red. She couldn't bring herself to start the fire.

"They go strange on you," Holland said. "It's not like they are stupid. It's just that they never had any chances to learn anything." The night was turning gray toward daylight, and they were driving slowly along the muffled side streets, only a couple of blocks from his house and the jailhouse across the way. "What you have to remember," Holland said, "with people who have gone crazy or wherever they have gone, is that they are like animals. There is nothing like a human being in there."

At least the snow had stopped. His gray two-story house with the towering Colorado blue spruce in front looked like no one had ever come or gone from it this night. The heavy snowfall had buried even his own tracks. All the windows were dark, there was that to think about. Doris always left a light on in the living room. An untouched world in the morning. Holland parked in the driveway and reached over and slapped Billy on the knee. "We are going to tell them stories," he said, "when this mud is settled."

Up there at the Frantz place he had carved his name over the mantel. "Funny how you would never do that in your own house," Holland said. Billy didn't answer. Holland tried to think of something in this house, his house, where he had lived since the year he was eleven, something that would seem as real to his memory as touching that sandstone and carving those initials. He shut off the idling pickup. How do you go to your own house when something has gone bad on the inside, when it doesn't seem like your place to live anymore, when you almost cannot recall living there although it was the place where you mostly ate and slept for all your grown-up life? Try to remember two or three things about living there. Try to remember cooking one meal.

"There is no use stalling on it," Billy said. "This time I am taking the shotgun. We got to go in there after him."

"You take the front," Billy said. "They won't suspect you. I'll cover the back. You give me a key to the back door, and I'll come around on them."

"What?"

"I'll cover the back."

"You just sit quiet," Holland said. "You leave that shotgun where it is, and you sit here quiet. There is nothing wrong in there, and if there is, I am not having you and that shotgun in my house."

"Is that an order?"

"Yes," Holland said, "that is an order. You will sit here quiet and I will go inside and turn on the lights, and then I will wave to you from the door, and you will not bring the shotgun. That is an order."

So there it was. Doris and that kid, side by side and sleeping, like no one would ever come up the creaking stairs a step at a time with a pistol drawn, to shoot them in that bed where he had always slept until now. Sometimes there is no choice but to walk into your own house. Far away, you think, and you do not want to see. You come home and you say do not tell me. You say, I have hunted the elk all over the snowfields of the Selway, and I do not want to know what happened here. And then there is a morning you walk in and take a look in your own house, like any traveler.

The .38 Detective Special was cold as a rock in his hand, and

Holland thought: I could kill them, one and two and done with, except for being an old man alone down there in that living room, and the explanations.

"Are they there?" It was Billy, whispering loud from the bottom of the stairway. Billy with his own .38 Detective Special in his hand. You could walk away, down the stairs, and tell Billy no. You could tell Billy no and go across to the jail and start making telephone calls, to the coroner and the state police, and come back here later, and say you don't know how you missed them, you don't understand how they could have been here all the time in your own house, and overlooked.

"Yeah," Holland said, and his voice was loud and harsh. "Yeah, they are sure as hell here. You ought to see them here. You come on up and see them." Holland switched on the bedroom lights as they came fighting awake under the bedclothes to see him standing with that black pistol in his hand, the bearded kid and Doris, her face soft and old without the eyeglasses, Doris sitting up and her breasts flat and naked, hanging and empty in the way she never let him see. Holland just stood there, giving them some time to figure out who they were going to be this morning.

"If this ain't hell," Holland said, when Doris just went on sitting there uncovered, her eyes out of focus without the eyeglasses. "I always figured it would be me," Holland said. "Some one of these whiskey tramps would come in and find me shacking down with his lady, and I would be sitting there wondering if he would shoot, and when." He could hear Billy coming up the stairs, one step at a time.

"Billy," Holland said, "forget it. Go on back down. We will all be down in a minute. I'm coming down." Holland turned back to the bed.

"The two of you get dressed," Holland said, "and then you come down the stairs and we will have some coffee and talk about what is going to happen next." Holland went over and shook the kid's clothing to make sure there was no gun, and then he left them.

But that was a mistake. At the bottom of the stairs he knew it was a mistake. Racked in the corner of his closet there was the 30-30 his father had left, and the scope-sighted 30-06 Holland carried while hunting mule deer and elk, and the two shotguns, the 12-gauge for Canada geese and mallards, and the 20-gauge for brush birds, pheasant and quail and the chuckers he had one time hunted down on the far desert rimrock country of southeastern Oregon, near the Nevada border on the bare sagebrush mountains. And there were stacks of boxed shells alongside the weapons.

With Billy hovering behind him while he made coffee in the kitchen, Holland knew he had made the bad mistake and tried to think about something else. There was no use going back up the stairs, either the kid had one of the shotguns or he didn't. And sure enough, he did. When Holland turned from plugging in the coffee, the kid was standing there in the doorway to the kitchen, barefoot and naked except for his pants, holding the 12-gauge. Doris stood behind him, wrapped in a blanket. Billy had turned useless again, standing by the electric stove with his arms reaching upward, pointing the .38 at the ceiling. Holland raised his own hands. "You stay calm," Holland said, "and we will give up our weapons, and we will all have us a cup of coffee with sugar and cream to get us warm."

"Billy," Holland said, "bring down the weapon very slowly, aiming it toward the window, and drop it in the sink."

"And Doris," Holland said, "you come over here and you pick my weapon out of my holster, and you take both mine and Billy's and you throw them out the back door into the snow. Then we will be all right, and we will have some coffee."

Except for the gun, it was like a holiday, or one of those Sundays after a winter dance with people sleeping over, when everyone wakes up half drunk and that is fine because there is nothing to do but sit around the kitchen and sip coffee with no thought that Monday is coming. Four cups of steaming coffee and the gray morning light through the windows, and only the kid tipped back in his chair with one of the .38 Police Special pistols in his hand to mar the scene. "If you won't shoot," Holland said, "I would get a shot of whiskey from under the sink. There is another bottle under there."

"The whiskey is in the living room," Doris said, "on the mantel. We had some last night. He was shaking and dying."

"Well then, you get the bottle for me," Holland said. "Please, or he will shoot me if I try to get it for myself."

"What you might think," Doris said, "is not true. He needed body warmth. He was dying of cold. You can understand that."

"I understand that," Holland said. "Body warmth and dying of cold. Why don't you get me the whiskey, and we will all feel better in a little while."

"No," the kid said, when Doris had gone for the whiskey, "we won't feel any better. My sister is dead, you saw them, they are all dead up there, and no whiskey is going to make us feel any better."

"We could have some whiskey in our coffee anyway," Holland said. "We have all been out in the cold, and the whiskey can't hurt."

"That's right," the kid said, and for the first time his eyes did not slide away from Holland's. "We all been out in the cold. There's a way you get sick when you been too long out in the cold, not so much freezing or anything as just shivering and you can't think. The part to notice first is that you can't think right. There is a name for it, Danzig knew the name, and you can die from it. Last night when I came in here I couldn't think right, and she took care of me. That's all there was. The cure is dry clothing and body warmth. There is a name for it."

"That woman," Holland said, "I don't know what she made of you but you got to understand she is an old woman. Just yesterday she was not an old woman, but now she is. There is all kinds of ways to go sick. Just thinking about all those dead people can make you go strange."

"Danzig knew the name for it," the kid said.

"Danzig taught you plenty, didn't he?" Holland said.

"There was one thing that was good about Danzig," the kid said, tipping his chair forward, sitting with his elbows on his knees, the .38 Police Special aimed at Holland as Doris came back with the whiskey bottle, "and that was that he knew things."

"Go ahead," the kid said, motioning at the whiskey bottle with the pistol, "go ahead and pour. Some whiskey would be all right for you. You been out like I was. But you got to understand there was something wrong with Danzig. He wanted the right things, but there was something wrong.

"When I was growing up," the kid said, "you knew my father. His name was Mac Banta, and he lived down there in the Bitterroot."

"I never knew anybody named Banta," Holland said.

"Well, he was there anyway," the kid said, "and there was those spring mornings with the geese flying north, and I would stand out on the lawn with the sun just coming up and the fence painted white around my mother's roses, and it would be what my father called a bluebird morning. That is what Danzig wanted, bluebird mornings. My sister would be there, and my mother and my father, and the birds playing in the lilac. Comes down to a world of hurt was what my father would say, and he would laugh because nothing could hurt you on those bluebird mornings. And that is what Danzig wanted."

Holland poured the whiskey and sat there in his kitchen, the four of them around the oak kitchen table while the kid talked and fondled the .38, all of them but the kid sipping at the coffee and whiskey and listening while the kid told them about Danzig, and Danzig's money, and the way Danzig was going to stop everything with those automatic rifles and snowmobiles and the closed-circuit television, seeing there was no need for anything but bluebird mornings. "But he lost interest," the kid said, "and after a while it was like he was just playing. After a while all any of them were doing up there was just smoking dope and fucking."

The kid named Banta turned to look at Doris. "I am sorry

for saying that," he said, "but that is all any of them were doing up there, smoking dope and fucking. There is no other way to say it. That is when I left. My sister, Grace, she wouldn't go, she was worse than any of them, so I left her there.

"And now she is dead," Banta said, "and she cried. I could see the tears on her face. But it was Danzig who should have cried."

"Boy," Holland said, "let me show you something. Out there on the seat of my pickup there is a carving. You let me show you that carving. You let Doris go out and get me that carving, and I will show you something."

They stood by the picture window in the living room and watched Doris go out barefoot in the snow and open the pickup with her blanket wrapped around her like some native woman and come back with the soap bear. In the kitchen they sat back around the oak table while the kid stared at the face of the carving, the intricate fangs of the soap bear, and the fine etched ruff of hair over the hump. "Now let me show you something," Holland said, and he took the carving from the boy and carried it to the sink. Holland turned on the hot water, and let it go until it was steaming, and held the head of the bear under the flow, and then with his hands burning he began to rub and wash at the slippery foaming soap until the tiny etched lines were gone and the carving was mostly gone, until there was nothing but the smooth wet surface of what had been as precise and as perfect as that girl could make it be. Holland held the dripping object out toward the boy. "Now you look at this," Holland said. "You have come in here and you have ruined some things of mine, and now I have ruined what your sister was doing that you did not know a thing about. Every mark your sister made is slicked away. So you lift up your head and shoot me if you think you can, but there is one thing about it, and that is that we are even right now. You have done me some damage, coming into my house like you have, and I have done you some damage, but maybe you have the best of it because some morning you might come to see that nobody ever did owe you any bluebirds, not ever. But maybe that same morning you might see that the best bluebird you ever had was that soap bear, and it washed away so easy. So we are even. You shoot me if you got the notion, but I am willing to call it even.

"Or what you could do," Holland said, "is get up and walk out of this kitchen and out of here. There is a chance you could go upstairs and get into your clothes while we all sit around this table, and you could leave. If you are smart at all, that is what you will do. If you didn't leave any absolutely fresh prints up with those dead people nobody will ever be able to pin you with all that mess, and you will get away free. If you shoot me you will have to shoot everyone here, and you are a dead man then. You have wiped your sister clean, and you have got Danzig clean, but there is no way you can get everything to stay clean. Maybe you ought to just leave things go the way they are for a while, and walk out. People like you," Holland said, "are always forgetting the ghosts there are in this world."

"There is too much," the kid said, "you don't forget. You start letting those things go and you are not anybody. You got it painted on the outside of your jailhouse. When I was a kid in high school we laughed about that, and Danzig, he laughed about that. A new world every morning. Wake up and nothing counts from yesterday.

"And you know what?" the kid said. "That is bullshit. You know what they were doing up there? You know what my sister did for Christmas? She cooked three turkeys. And you know what she did? She painted them all green with food coloring. Did you ever think about eating a green turkey? Did you ever see green stuffing? Green birds for a green world was what she said, like turkeys should be the color of grass. Springtime turkeys is what she called them. That is what you end up with. A new world every morning, and you got green turkeys." The kid went on tapping the table with the pistol barrel, leaving tiny marks in the polished hardwood surface.

"It was a joke," Holland said. "The sign was a joke."

"Well, the fun is over," the kid said.

"Not just yet." It was Billy Kumar, and he held a palm-sized one-shot gambler's gun of the kind Holland had seen only in Western movies. From somewhere in his clothing, while the kid preached at Holland, Billy had come out with that tiny weapon, with a chrome-plated barrel only about an inch and a half long, and he held it aimed straight at the side of the kid's head, dead on Virgil Banta from three or four feet. All this time, Holland thought, he had been packing that thing hidden.

"We got one more piece of fun," Billy Kumar said, and even though his hand was trembling just so slightly, Billy didn't look frightened, not even angry, but more like a great door had just swung wide and he was seeing the first thing he ever liked in his life, his eyes squinted and lips pulled back, and chewing at just the tip of his tongue. "You drop that pistol. Just open your hand and let it drop."

"Billy," Holland said. "Wait a minute."

"I am going to kill the old man," Virgil Banta said, not moving. "On the count of three I am going to kill the old man."

Billy almost missed. His one shot struck Virgil Banta in the shoulder, but that was enough. The kid didn't even fire. Maybe that is to his credit, Holland thought later, maybe he didn't mean to fire. But at the time, as Holland rolled sideways out of his chair, knowing there would be a second explosion of fire in the room, directly in his face, the shot that never came, he was thinking he had killed himself. All my life, he was thinking, knowing Billy was beyond his control even before the shot. All my life, Holland was thinking, waiting for this, some cockeyed son of a bitch getting me killed. All my life getting myself killed.

"He thought you would understand," Doris said, "that was why he came here, thinking you would understand."

"What am I to understand?" Holland said. "He is up there in my bedroom jackass naked, along with you, and I am supposed to make something wonderful out of that? He was a murderer, and he was crazy.

"But then forget it," Holland said. "Which is what I mean – forget it. This is all something to forget."

It was late darkening afternoon; and the blood had been scrubbed from the kitchen floor; and the Banta kid was safe in the county hospital with federal deputies guarding him; and Billy Kumar was gone home with his pearl-handled one-shot Las Vegas gambler gun, gone home to be a new man; and Shirley Holland was at his kitchen table again, picking at a bacon-and-mushroom omelet. Thick country bacon, and none of those canned mushrooms, the real mushrooms Doris gathered down on the sandy riverbanks of the Clark Fork in spring just as the cottonwoods were coming into fresh leaf. Real mushroom frozen for winter. One cup of coffee, Holland thought, and then I will go to sleep. Outside the window over the sink, snow was falling thick again. "What could I have understood?" Holland said, and he wondered what those children thought as they scrubbed the soot off a sandstone mantelpiece where someone had carved a heart with the letters S H inside. What did they understand?

"Nothing," Doris said, "It's just what he thought, he thought you would understand. Nothing happened up there. I swear. Holland?"

"Fine," Holland said. "The first good spring day, a warm day, I am going to paint out that sign. You get to be my age, and a thing like that isn't anything you want to think about seriously."

Doris didn't even look around from where she was rinsing the frying pan.

"Nothing happened," Doris said.

"It never does."

Blue Stone

OLD MAN TRAINER, they say, has finally gone.

As he rides his Italian ten-speed bicycle down the long slope of curving asphalt roadway toward Red Branch, the farm women watch from their orchards, from screened veranda porches, and they say it: he's gone crazy. They shake their heads sadly. So great a man, they say, and now he's gone. He's loopy, they say.

Dropping toward the concrete bridge over the Bitterroot River, timbered mountains to the west already bluish in the midsummer glare, resplendent in his white tennis outfit while waves of heat distort the sky over the tan brick buildings at the center of town, Trainer imagines tranquility and evening. He invents that other life which he has lately imagined as so possibly his – a small lake in wilderness highlands with water unruffled under orange clouds at sunset, absolutely still. A surface marked only by the circular dimplings of trout sucking down insects.

So as he wheels down the highway there's this lake in Trainer's mind. Against the far shore, almost invisible in the gray of twilight, a small boat rocks quietly. The man in the boat is Trainer.

Standing on a boulder large as a child's bed, at the end of a steep and rocky point, Trainer does not know the names of trees around him, just that they are evergreen; but he is apprehensive about the man in the boat. The boat has no motor, and the man is rowing slowly, with great deliberation, as an old and tired man would.

Trainer smiles into the wind because he is only old, not tired, and he is pedaling swiftly over the bridge crossing the Bitter-root River. Not tired, not at all tired.

But how reassuring it would be to imagine the soft puttering of a trolling motor, three or four horsepower motor. Across the still water the sound would float at somewhere near the human pulse rate, and ease the loneliness of an old, tired man. With a motor the man would be able to extricate himself from trouble. But there is no motor.

Coasting, Trainer comes off the bridge. Weight on the handlebars, he pedals again, lifting the pedals with his toe clamps. Pushing down with the balls of his feet. Sweating easily. He circles before the Rexall Drug and then stops and chains his bicycle to a lamppost. He stands for a minute cooling himself in the breeze before entering the barroom.

"Beautiful," Trainer says, skirting the shuffleboard table.

"One thing," he says, "you can count on every time."

The bartender stares out a window shielded by Venetian blinds. Rubbing his soft palms together, the bartender leans his bulk against the back bar and picks at his teeth with a plastic straw. His cheeks flutter.

Trainer hopes the old man is fishing. Plotting against some huge trout. Trainer can see the old man's features now, substantial as the Miller High Life sign rotating over the Men's Room doorway. Trainer can see the hands, the face which is soft as a child's, whiskerless and even more aged than Trainer had imagined.

The bartender turns the stiff cuffs of his mended white shirt up over his forearms.

Looking back from the prow of the boat where the May flies cluster, Trainer watches the old man gently rowing, his hands dark and fragile as tobacco-colored leaves.

"Going to start a circus," Trainer says.

The bartender grins and fires his plastic straw into the garbage like a dart. "So you said," the bartender says. "You said you was going to do that."

The old man is fishing with a split bamboo fly rod, unsuitable for trolling but beautifully made, of Tonkin bamboo. No doubt his favorite among the rods he owns. The oarlocks give a slight creaking sound, which in some measure makes up for the absence of a motor. But not really. A motor would take him home. Trainer imagines the old man turning some knob and the boat lifting gracefully from the water and diving south over the horizon, the old man's face torn by wind and anticipation as he clears the first mountains.

"Going to fill it up with crazies," Trainer says. "Bring in people from California to see it. I know plenty who would. Going to fly 'em in. Jet planes. Maybe helicopters the last stretch.

"Going to make a fortune," Trainer says.

"Rich get richer," Trainer says.

The bartender shakes his head seriously. "No harm in some fun," he says.

"You know me," Trainer says.

"No," the bartender says. It's true. Even though Trainer has taken to coming here each day, this man remains a stranger, this dark empty room not a place Trainer truly remembers. Not like he remembers the blue pure water of a lake he's never seen.

"But you do know me," Trainer says. Because it's also true Trainer is the richest man in this valley, the most famous man in this state, even if an outlander. An old man now, reduced to reinventing himself, who once starred in 157 Western movies. A make-believe past Trainer does not much remember.

The old man on the lake is trolling with a fly rod, and it's rigged out with a lovely and expensive fly reel, a Hardy, British, and a white nylon fly line. An outfit unsuitable for trolling. The old man is in love with a sporting life. The man is old and has decided to go with his finest gear. A nice story, Trainer thinks.

"How about a Bloody Mary?" Trainer says. "With no Mary."

The bartender pours tomato juice from a gray plastic pitcher, dumps out the first glass. "That one had a fly in it," he says. "Makes you sick to think about," he says.

"Not me," Trainer says. "I like 'em."

The fisherman's clothing is worn, a sweat-stained gray hat, tattered Levi jacket and high-heeled work boots of badly scuffed kangaroo; and his lake is a heart-stopping blue, as if this water existed only in an advertisement for vacations in New Zealand, a lake hidden below mountains on the southern island. Trainer gulps his juice.

"Wish them crazies would come in," Trainer says.

"Never can tell," the bartender says. "They keep their own schedules."

As if to disprove him, the outside door bangs open, but it's not the people Trainer expects. It's a woman and two men. The smaller of the men, middle-aged and hump-shouldered in paint-flecked coveralls and a peaked black cap, shuffles toward the rear of the bar, head swinging from side to side until, grunting and wheezing, he mounts a stool and turns to glare up the bar toward Trainer. The woman and the tall man stand in the doorway.

"You going to behave?" the bartender shouts.

"I ain't good enough?" The hump-shouldered man's voice is oddly pitched, almost a screech, as he digs a green plastic coin purse from his pocket and holds up a silver dollar. "This ain't good enough?"

"Not when you act like you do," the bartender says.

"Not when your sister sucks grapes." The hump-shouldered man grins down the bar at Trainer. "Seedless grapes," he says.

The bartender sets him up a short beer. "Close the door," he says to the couple in the doorway. "You let in the heat."

"Seedless grapes," the hump-shouldered man repeats, and then he sips the froth from his beer without touching the glass. The tall man at the door reminds Trainer of a chicken hawk. Hooked nose and no chin.

"Put me to mind of someone I used to know," Trainer says.

"Animal man down in Hollywood." The woman – thin with a man's white shirt tied into a halter under heavy breasts, red hair out from her face like a halo and her face covered with freckles the size of pennies – the woman slams the door.

"Cat man," Trainer says. "Lions and tigers."

Trout break the slick surface of lake-water. Reeds and tules, water lilies, grow near the marshy shore and threaten to surround the boat. The white line trails out behind. Darkness is coming. The boat eases along amid the water-flowers. Fish are no longer rising. Over the old man's shoulder a horizon of stubby peaks reaches into the sunlight.

"This is my closest relation," the woman says. The tall man stands uncertainly beside her, gulping as though to work a mossy thing from his throat.

"My sister's brother," the woman says. "Half-brother to me. Step-brother. What you want to call it."

The bartender pours her a double bourbon, water back. "Winnie," he says. "I see him. What's he drink?"

"Buttermilk," the tall man says. "Or regular, if that's all you got."

"Day-old cream," the bartender says, "is what I got."

"How about a bottle of pop?" the woman says. "Bottle of pop wouldn't slow you down," she says to this tall man.

"Anything," the tall man says, "that don't bother my sensations."

"You ever have anything to do with cats?" Trainer says.

"This here is Wesley Matchless," the woman says.

The bartender sets a bottle of ginger ale on the counter. Trainer pulls a crumpled five dollar bill from the pocket of his white tennis shorts. "Matchless," he says. "Never heard of that name."

"I made it up," the tall man says. "It's my traveling name. Picked it myself."

Trainer throws the five dollar bill out on the counter. "I'll get those," he says.

"You're all right," the woman says.

"Just trying to please," Trainer says.

"That's the trouble," the tall man says, staring into the mirror, meeting Trainer's eyes. "Trying to please."

"Yeah," the bartender says, coming back with the change, "that's bad trouble all right."

"It is," the tall man says. "That's why I come here. I come here to meet you." He points a long, crooked finger at Trainer. "You're the man."

"Hitchhiked," the woman says. "From Rawlings. Overnight."

"I got a circus act," the tall man says. "Least I had one. Had to give it up. Too much of that trying to please."

"He lights fires with his breath," the woman says. "No matches." Her pale green eyes glisten.

"Wesley," she says, "is a master."

"Well," Trainer says, "I ain't hiring yet.

"Actually," Trainer says, "I'm meeting some other people. Not really interested in professional acts.

"This is an all-amateur show," Trainer says.

"That's just it," the tall man says. "None of that trying to please. Just a nice amateur life." He smiles at Trainer, his mouth a toothless gash under his hooked nose.

"No professionals," Trainer says firmly.

"What I told you," the hump-shouldered man screeches from the far end of the bar, "is he's hiring crazies." He grins, and raises his half-empty beer glass. "Not just damned fools."

"Denton," the woman says. "You shut up. There's plenty of trouble without you." She touches Trainer's bare elbow. "Denton," she says, "is probably crazy. Maybe Denton is who you're looking for."

"What I'm after," Trainer says, "is a syndicate." There's in him a deep sense of relief as that word comes out. Another discovery. "Syndicate," he says again, softly, the word soothing, a name for what they will be. The something syndicate. The what syndicate? It will come, Trainer thinks, it will come. It makes sense.

"There'll be others," Trainer says. "Don't worry."

"All the way from Rawlings," the woman says. "Overnight."

"Denton," the woman says, nodding at the hump-shouldered man, "don't believe in nothing. He is a disbeliever."

"But you haven't seen them other folks," Trainer says. "The old woman and the girl and them two boys with cap pistols and stick horses?"

"I look for them to come wandering along," Trainer says. Those harmless people without ambitions. Only a few mornings before he'd seen them again, straggling toward town on the hot asphalt, the four of them thin and dark as ever, faces narrow as heads of birds and eyes as blank; and it was then he came to his idea, recognizing he'd seen them numberless times before. They'd always been somewhere waiting, preserved like flies in home-canned jelly.

"After all," the woman says, "Wesley did come all the way."

"We'll see," Trainer says. "In due time." They came with the old woman, the mother, in the lead, hard-faced and mute. Then the two boys, already middle-aged and simple to distract as children, unshaven under formless black hats and mounted on stick-horses with plastic heads, firing toy pistols at the passing automobiles. Trailing another hundred yards behind came the sister, Norgene, illegally sterilized by the county physician when she was thirteen, after her second pregnancy aborted. Both times knocked up by her brothers, or at least so it was claimed. And by that sterilization given freedom to screw anyone she wanted for any money they'd give her. That much was common knowledge. Most often any country boy with a dollar bill.

With his bicycle propped against a motel office, after plugging nickels into the soft drink machine, the cold bottle slick as a river stone in his fingers, Trainer saw into the hollowness of her dark eyes, saw something to envy — which was maybe just the obviousness of the idea there was nothing to be done, a strum of recognition, useless as that in the diamond-red eyes of roadside animals in the night, that flicker of red as the light passes, even in the eyes of jackrabbits.

"You see," Trainer says, "we been in the same business."

"What's that?" the tall man said, squinting with concentration.

"Good times."

"I didn't have no fun."

"That's it," Trainer says. "You're professional. This deal don't want no professionals."

As if it might be possible that there's nothing more to be said on the matter, the tall man leaves his ginger ale on the counter, walks outside and gently closes the door behind him. "You wait," the woman says. "You just wait. You'll see something like you never seen."

So they wait, the bartender tapping the bottles along the back bar with a plastic stir-stick. They wait until the tall man comes back with a one-gallon can of gasoline. "This here," the tall man says, "could be your final number."

He tells Trainer how at the end of each performance he would light one of the crazies afire. "We'd put 'em in an asbestos suit," he says, "and then put some clown clothes over that. Just a little gasoline on them clown clothes. Then I come out in my all-red fireman's costume. There's drums, and then I shoot 'em with fire. Watch 'em blaze. An all amateur act."

The hump-shouldered man at the far end of the bar is screeching with laughter. "Denton," the woman says, "is a heretic."

The bartender shakes his head.

Trainer stares at himself in the blue mirror over the back bar, and scratches his belly. He glares into the lake where his old man is no longer fishing. The tall man pours the gasoline over his own head, stands drenched in that flammable, corrosive liquid. The tall man stands sputtering, eyes tightly closed. "This here," he says, "is what you do."

Trainer steps carefully from his stool, the floor far below and a terrible distance to fall. Haystacks are yellowing on a clear October day. Near the stream that enters the lake, a cluster of luridly bright aspen shimmer in the breeze. The tall man blinks and rubs at his eyes, which must be burning horribly.

Outside a brown canvas tent, Trainer looks toward the sunset while a white butterfly lies damply crushed in his palm. He steps forward through the cool near-evening light, moves quickly and accurately as an acrobat negotiating distances between rooftops; and his clenched fist catches the sloping underside of that tall man's mouth, the impact with bone slow and firm until the tall man is wheeling backward into staggering collapse, arms flailing. It is the only time in all the staged fights of his life Trainer has not pulled the punch.

He tastes the salty blood from his cut knuckle.

The spilled gasoline has soaked into the dry flooring. The tall man is gasping. "See," he blubbers, "it's the real item."

The birch leaves are turning yellow and dropping after each cold night. Every morning there's a rim of thin ice around the canvas bucket. The lake lies still as a blue mirror polished by a woman's slender white fingers.

"You ain't burning nobody," Trainer says. The man they call Denton is laughing again as Trainer turns the turquoise ring around on his finger, silver fluting surrounding the stone. That ring he will trail through the water as the boat moves ever so slowly. High in wilderness mountains.

Momentum Is Always the Weapon

THE RADIO from Winnemucca predicted rain over the high desert of northern Nevada for the next two days. Now delicate sheets of lightning flared between the rimrocks, and the summer evening was darkened and freshened, great drops splattering into the dust and the odors of wet sage and manure mingling as the old man, Ambler, rode from the corral.

Christy was dead at twenty-three. The old man could not think about her except to see her as she had been when she was ten years old and laughing, her dark hair cropped off above her ears and her sharp face burned by the sun and wind. In the barn he had saddled the gelding quietly and mechanically, gathering the things he would need and pulling on the stiff, cold slicker, strapping the saddlebags onto the gelding and the scabbard for the thirty-thirty. Then he damped out the erratic light from the kerosene lantern and climbed up into his saddle and left.

The wind came in sudden gusts, rattling the rain off his hard slicker. The rain was coming more heavily and the wind settled into a steady blow. He managed to light his pipe and settled himself in the saddle, smelling the aroma of the rough-cut tobacco and seeing only the small glow of the pipe.

There was a fence and then a gate, and the old man got down and led the gelding through, and then set off on a pair of narrow wagon tracks that led directly away from the fence. The tracks curved up gently through the rising sand hills on an old trail tramped by the antelope and mustangs and Paiutes. Finally the horse began to climb, stumbling in the gravel and rock where the wagon tracks had been eroded into small gullies.

Ambler could smell the sour wet mahogany brush that grew in clumps under the rimrocks, and then the land leveled out and he pulled the horse in and rested sideways in the saddle, easing himself.

Far out below he could see the first glimmerings of light from the house, light from the uncurtained windows flickering through what he knew were the leaves of the long row of Lombardy poplar trees. The wagon track came out on a new road, and fresh gravel crunched under the hooves of the gelding. About a hundred yards from the house there was a lull in the wind, a silence, and then a half-dozen hounds came baying and yelping toward him. The old man clapped the rommal clapper on the tree of his saddle and sent the gelding leaping forward, and then just short of the fence he jerked the horse up and was off him, talking to the animal, soothing him while the dogs yipped.

The front door to the house opened. The man in the doorway shouted once at the dogs and sent them around the corner of the house. The only sounds now were the hum of the Delco power plant and splatter of rain and wind. The tall young man came from out of the doorway, far enough to see who it was. "Jesus Christ, Walt," he said.

Old man Ambler had the gelding under control, and stepped forward, leading him easily by the reins. "Hello, Barry," he said. "Christy died yesterday."

"What are you talking about? Let's put that horse away."

They bedded the horse in the small slope-roofed shed that passed as a barn. When they were through, the boy stopped in the doorway of the shed, looking across the lot toward the house. He lighted a cigarette. "What about Christy?" he said finally.

"I need a place to sleep," the old man said.

"There's nobody in Eddie's room. He went to town a week ago, and ain't got enough of it to suit him yet. Sooner or later I'll have to go get him."

They went across the muddy lot toward the house, toward

the light that gleamed across the puddles. Inside the back screen door the young man helped Ambler out of his slicker and chaps and hung them on pegs along the back wall. Sitting outside in the rain were three nearly new cars and an old pick-up truck with the side windows knocked out.

Going into the light and warmth of the kitchen, Ambler was blinded momentarily. The youngest of the brothers, the young man who'd been helping him, said, "Guess you know everybody, Walt."

"Close enough," Ambler said, and he did, remembered all of them, the three brothers and the missing one. Even the old hired man, he remembered him from someplace. The eldest of them, John, who ran the business, got up and waved him to a seat in front of the oil stove and took his mackinaw coat and said, "Sit and warm yourself. Nora can get you coffee and a plate of food."

Three women sat around the room, two young ones who were knitting and the old woman, Nora, the mother of the boys. Ambler nodded at each of them in turn and then sat in front of the stove. The older woman got up and went to the stove where she filled a plate with meat and potatoes leftover from the evening meal.

One of the boys had been playing a guitar. He stopped and let his fingers run softly over the strings. Grinning uneasily, he slapped his hands on the box of the instrument and moved to hang it on the wall. "Too much static for the radio," he said. The sound of the wind was muted inside the building, but Ambler could hear it as he ate and the family silently watched.

"Maybe you wonder why I come over here all of a sudden," the old man said, when he had handed his plate back to the woman. "Six years since I come into this house the last time. I was going to kill Eddie. Tonight I had the same idea. What happened was Christy got killed Saturday night. She never come home from the time she run off with Eddie. But now it's all done with and I want you people to know I don't care any more, and to finish this off with no more trouble." The old man lit his pipe again when he was through talking, staring down into the bowl while he worked at it.

"We got no manners." The oldest brother dug into the cupboard under the sink, and came up with a half-full bottle of bourbon. One of the young women put five heavy glass tumblers on the table. After his drink the hired man rose without speaking and went off upstairs and could be heard moving around his room and then dropping his boots and rolling into bed. The eldest son showed old man Ambler to his room – an unpainted and unadorned place above the stairs.

"We're all sorry she's dead, Walt." The man spoke quietly. He had his hand on the doorknob and was half in and half out of the room. "She was the best there was around here, Walt, but I can't see where it was Eddie that spoiled her."

The old man sat on the bed. "Maybe not."

"Could be you set her up higher than she was. Just the two of you for so long." The man, Eddie's brother, closed the door and left Ambler alone in the room.

The old man heaped his things onto a chair and dropped his boots among the scattered gear of the absent younger son who had six years ago run off with Christy and then dumped her completely when the sheriff brought them back from Reno after three weeks. The old man pulled the string on the single bare light bulb and was surprised the radium dial alarm clock showed the time to be after midnight.

Lying quiet he was aware of the drumming of the rain that was being driven against the slanting roof above him. *Dead*, he thought. She has known everything for these last two days. He turned in the bed of the boy who had started her and wondered how it had been in the light and sharp-edged shadows out in the dust and tumbleweeds where the cars were parked around a country dance hall two hundred miles away, over near the foot of the Ruby Mountains. She had been shot square in the chest and dead before anyone knew better in a fight between two unknown drunken men. The pretty girl with the long black hair dead when they reached her – the deputy sheriff hung his head and told the story through once and then left, the dust from his going rising high in an alkali-colored rooster tail hanging far off in the afternoon stillness before the storm. Ambler stared at the raftered darkness and wished luck to the stranger who would dope out so many years in the state penitentiary for killing her, wished she could have been home just once lately, and wondered if he would have killed Eddie Matson with the thirty-thirty when it came right down to it. He tried to remember her and wished he had a photo of her taken in these last years because all he could remember was the long swinging hair tied with a red ribbon the last time she visited, and the pointed face of the little girl. He slept then, lulled by the whiskey and already sick of his own despair.

In the morning he ate with them, saddled the gelding, and rode off, his yellow slicker outlining him against the sage hills in rain. The rain soaked his hat and the brim drooped before his face. Water dropped in steady streams from the horse's mane. The animal kept its head down and picked easily through the natural paths in the sagebrush, plodding heavily. Far off through the sweeping slants of the storm the horizon lay flat with steps of rimrock in some places, but mostly he watched close beside the path the horse picked and saw the straggling grass which grew among the rocks was already greener. The feed would hold for the rest of the dry season. There was no wind. Dropping the reins over the saddle horn, he stuffed his hands into the pocket of his slicker. The horse continued to choose its own way.

At the rim of the canyon, Ambler climbed off. This trail was dangerous when dry and worse now, and there could be no reason to cripple a horse over this sort of foolishness. So the two of them slipped and stumbled down the trail until they were at the bottom of the dry prehistoric rivercourse, working upstream toward the cave and the spring. Around the little waterhole were a few scrub willow, and at the mouth of the cave, where the tiny stream came into daylight, the old man saw signs of watering livestock along with antelope and mule deer signs. Wild horses had used this hidden water until after the war, when they were run with airplanes and slaughtered for dog food.

The cave was broad as a large room. When the old man had unsaddled the gelding he hauled the saddle and bed into the mouth of the shelter and unrolled his tarp. He hobbled the horse in a sheltered place in the willows. Ambler smoked and made up his mind how to go about this last piece of business.

As the afternoon darkened he went down to the spring and drank and then went back to the bedroll and dug out a sack of dried venison jerky and cut slivers with his knife and munched slowly while the gray daylight faded into evening. The cave extended far into the darkness behind him and he could smell the warm and acrid odor of nesting animals, and hear the rustling of mice and squirrels and hear the dripping of the water that gathered to form the little spring. When he could no longer see, he pulled off his boots and climbed between the rough blankets and slept.

The bar was crowded two deep along the rail, and he edged through until the barkeep poured him a shot and scooped up his two bits. All through the crowd were riders with numbers pinned to the backs of their bright shirts.

Another drink. He sipped it slowly, quiet amid the ungainly and brawny women and the somber toothpick chewing men, then worked his way back to the sidewalk. Taking his key at the hotel desk he went up to his room, stopped before the door, and knocked. No answer. She was not there. On the bare frame dresser he found a note telling him she had gone downstairs to the coffee shop.

He lay on the bed, his feet propped over the end, his eyes wandering over the stark room. The woman had not settled anything. He rolled off the bed and walked to the window and leaned with his hands against the sill while he watched the crowd on the street. Men fished in their pockets for cigarette materials, their faces working and squinting while they talked, a line of gossiping country men with their feet propped on the high bumpers of beaten cars, pickups. Another group of men stood beside the entrance to the hotel – ranchers with cigars and engraved belts and business voices. The hot dog stand at the corner was surrounded with women and children. He watched them and looked for some clue to whatever mystery he was contemplating. Then he heard his new bride outside in the hallway, her quiet voice coming clearly through the transom.

Christy was dead.

Her mother: black hair and pale body bent as she watched herself in some long bedroom mirror, her ribs showing through the flesh, and the thing that fascinated him, the winding of the long hair in the tight coil she made for sleeping. And then the birth, their only child. The woman had lain awake at night beside him and taken to disregarding him. Then she rode off in the middle of a summer day, on the best saddle mare he ever owned, leaving the seven-year-old girl for him to discover in the evening light, sitting on the front steps and waiting.

Ambler was awake. The rain had stopped. To the east there was a strip of clear and intense blue sky between the horizon and the layer of clouds. His horse was off cropping grass below the water hole. The grass and sage were heavy with moisture, and the air was chilled and fresh.

After a while Ambler sat up and pulled on his boots, shivering. He ate more of the jerky. Then he went out and caught the horse and pulled off the hobbles and sent the startled animal off at a run with a slap on its haunches.

Back in the cave he loaded the thirty-thirty, wondering while he did if he should wash himself or at least clean his mouth with some of the spring water, and then he thought to hell with it and wondered if he should pray or something and then laughed at himself.

Maybe these things are not enough, he thought, and he lifted the thirty-thirty, weighing it in his grasp, a relic of older and

better times. As he laid the rifle on the bedroll a glint of dark
white back in the shadows of the cave caught his eye. It was the
skull of a badger, lying among remnants of bone and hide,
picked clean by the mice and ants and identifiable only by the
scraps of fur.

Ambler examined the tiny and delicate structure of the
bones in the skull as though it were something never seen before and looked closely at the way the teeth were fastened to
the jawbone, built for hanging on. You are a hapless fool, he
thought, and unloaded the rifle and rolled it inside the bedroll.
He heaped his possessions on a ledge inside the cave and began
the long walk home.

It was evening of the second day before he reached the home
place. The gelding was waiting for him, cropping grass outside
the first gate. The sun had set and all around him were the quiet
movements of small animals. The old man fixed himself a meal
and watched the air outside his windows darken and cool. He
went to bed and slept. Then for no reason other than the rasping of his own breath, he was awake and opening his eyes to
the board wall. He turned in the bed, thinking he would be
awake now and unable to sleep, but even while turning notic-
ing the oddness. The window across the room was light from
the moon, and around the window there was the deep and
solid yellow light, and as he saw it there was a compelling
sensation of *person* – some other thing sharing the room with
him.

Without surprise he saw a figure leaning against the wall,
regarding him, and then it turned to the window. For a moment in the moonlight there was a face silhouetted, a profile of
someone who he might have known, once, no ghost but a face
he could almost catch a name for, a haggard woman, and then
it was gone and Ambler felt it all slipping away, like something
dreamed. *Who is this?* he thought.

The old man sank in the bed and turned to face the wall and
wondered whatever had happened to him, or tried to happen,

what thing had been revealed which he could not understand
or feel anything toward except revulsion. He could not remember the face, just that he had seen a face, and some terrible
nervousness of energy was trembling through him.

The rest of the night he lay awake. Toward daybreak he rose
and built a fire in the kitchen and made coffee and drank it
heavy with sugar and condensed milk. It was warm and it
helped calm him. Finally he made breakfast, venison steak and
milk gravy, and after eating he cleaned the dishes and went to
sit in one of the big chairs in the main room of the house, chairs
he had hauled in from Elko, bought at auction after the old
Sheepman Hotel closed. With the full light of day he could
recall little of the experience of the night before, only that it
had happened.

For a long time he didn't work away from the house and the
corrals, the barn and his small meadows. He worked slowly at
the business of stockpiling his hay down by the windmill and
in the barn loft. As the days passed at the slow tasks, working
alone as he always had, Ambler tried to recapture what had
happened that night in the moonlight.

The summer began to fade and finally it was fall. He rode
out into the desert because it was necessary, and pushed his
cattle in toward the meadows so when the snow came they
would be home. Some days he worked in the barn, getting
ready for winter, mending harness and building new side racks
for the sled he used for feeding when the snow was down.

From the loft of the barn, looking east, breaking loose the
mud-dauber sparrows' nests with a shovel handle, Ambler saw
the bare-headed horseman climbing down to open the last
gate. Ambler watched the man close the wire gate, get back up
horseback on the gray roan gelding, and then he saw who it
was, Eddie Matson, the boy who had run off with Christy
those years ago. The only annoyance Ambler felt was at the
interruption of his solitude — just like a kid to be riding this
desert country without a hat, a red bandanna tied around his

forehead and draped down over his neck in the back as some kind of defense against the sun, which was, after all, in this fall season, no longer strong enough to bother.

But Eddie Matson was no longer a kid, he was unshaven and a man and close to thirty years old as Ambler looked up at him after climbing down from the barn loft. Whatever could be wrong with Eddie Matson was wrong. His eyes were mattering and squinted, like he had not slept, and his shotgun horsehide chaps were out at the knees, worn through. Eddie Matson sucked at his lower lip, like he was tasting the feel of his whiskers. "By God," he said, "here I am."

Ambler nodded, but didn't answer, only walked off toward the house, listening to the slow footfalls of Eddie Matson's gelding as it followed. Ambler turned. "How long you been riding that horse? You had better turn him loose for a rest. There's oats in the saddle shed."

Inside the house, Ambler reheated the morning coffee and set out two cups and poured whiskey in each, while Eddie Matson watched. "You can sleep the night," Ambler said, "and rest that horse, and then you might as well be gone."

Only after they had finished the coffee, after Ambler had fried some bacon while Eddie Matson drank another cup of coffee, as Eddie chewed at his thick sandwich, the bacon between thick slices of bread, did they do any talking, and then it was Ambler who got it started. "You can break your ass on these things," he said, "once you get it going."

Eddie Matson nodded. "A number of things," he said. "You just run out of speed. Things go as far as they can go, and then they don't go any more."

"That's the truth, far as it carries. You tell me what you come here for."

Eddie Matson chewed at another mouthful, and wiped his mouth with the back of his hand. "That's hard to say. Just to say I'm sorry about Christy, but I never thought you were right. We went down to Reno, them deputies come and took her home. I never come to get her again, she wouldn't have stayed with me either, you know that, she never stayed here with you after that, much. You figure that's my fault, but I don't see it." With a cupped hand Eddie Matson brushed crumbs from the flowered oilcloth on the table, and looked across at Ambler, slate-colored eyes deep in themselves and intent on saying a thing that Eddie couldn't excuse himself from trying to say, which had to be most of why he was here. "She started herself – there is nobody else to blame."

"Sounds to me like you are making excuses for yourself," Ambler said. "We can all make excuses, and do things we hate, and if there's one thing, it's to quit doing that. I scared the piss out of myself a while back, it was nobody but me, and maybe now I have quit doing everything, but I've tried to quit doing things I hate." This talk, as it came from him, was forming, and Ambler wondered how much he meant what he was saying as he listened to himself, and what he had quit doing beyond trusting his nerve.

"Make you a deal," Ambler said. Eddie Matson looked away, and just shook his head, as if yes, there should be a deal. "You come live here on this place, when you think you can." Ambler wondered what it was he was offering.

Eddie Matson kept nodding yes, and looked back at Ambler, and this time his eyes had gone surface gray again. "You getting too old?"

Ambler got up and poured them both more of the bitter coffee, and more of the whiskey that stood on the table between them. "Not so much that as give out with it all."

"Soon as I get a chance," Eddie Matson said. "All right. There are things that could be done around here."

But there was never a chance. The last week in October the wind blew cold from the north, and the Indian summer was over and always the first thing Ambler did those days when he came in from work was stoke up the fire and thaw out. There were only a few days of sleet rain before the gray November day when the snow began to come down in the late afternoon. Ambler watched it and remembered his daughter.

She had followed him across the slippery meadows and he had taken her hand and helped her keep up while the half circles of dampness on the worn toes of her boots grew larger and she laughed and puffed in the frosty air and they watched her breath float away. There seemed too much of himself in these memories. He wondered if he was, as they had said, too much taken up with her, and then he thought to hell with them.

The next morning the new dry snow covered the ground and was falling straight and soft in absolute stillness. In the evening he got up from his chair exhausted, surprised to realize he had not eaten and must be hungry. He forced himself to build a fire and cooked a steak and baked potato and mixed gray milk gravy and cut bread, and then he sat down and ate slowly. When he finished eating he was warm and at peace, and he smoked and looked out to where the little creek that flowed in front of the house was carving through the new drifts. The spring will come early, he thought, and the feed will be good. I'll turn out early and go spend some time in town. With drowsiness softening his thoughts, he started toward the bedroom when he fell and lay two hours unconscious before he started to drag himself somewhere, and then he was dead, of natural causes.

They didn't discover him until Eddie Matson finally came along and found his few head of starving cattle walking the fence line and gnawing the posts. After some search they located the widow and she had the place sold at auction. It went to a feedlot outfit from the Imperial Valley in California, who were buying up land with water all along the western foothills of the Steens Mountains for summer range. Eddie Matson leased the house and lived there alone seven years, until he married one of the Lamar sisters from Bonanza and moved over near Klamath Falls. He always said, living out his later years (on the dairy farm his wife inherited), that Old Man Ambler had taught him one thing, although it was hard to name. Something like never looking to see the time of day, never owning a watch, always guessing by the look of the sun. And night, he said, and he laughed, night didn't count.

The Underground River

RED YOUNT, the deputy, took his time. While the cold November wind was moving like distant water through the tops of yellow-barked ponderosas, Cleve recollected last night's dream: a long-haired old man on a gray horse galloped down an undulating, grass-covered slope toward a creekside village, willow-thatch houses behind yellowing grain patches, aspens and evergreens beyond the water. Soundless, framed by fir boughs, shotgun upraised in the man's right hand, the horse galloped on.

"Lonnie never was sensible when he drank," Red Yount said, in the midst of saying all the rest. Cleve stared at the ground, inch-deep in pumice dust as loose and yellow as corn flour.

The sheriff in Donan had sent Red Yount out to Cleve's when the word came from Red Bluff: Lonnie had died the night before in the Tehama County drunk tank, which meant he had managed to live 123 days since coming of legal age and collecting his share of the tribal money. "Leastwise," Red Yount said, "you can afford to bury him."

Cleve nodded. The money had led to this: over forty-three thousand dollars which had been seven years drawing interest in a Portland bank. Cleve, who had been resisting two years, since his own twenty-first birthday, had given in to what seemed common sense and taken his money at the same time, an identical $43,639.42.

"What the hell," Red Yount said. His car was a year-old black Plymouth sedan. "Wasn't like a surprise. What do you think? You don't say nothing."

"I was remembering how he acted in jail," Cleve said. "He stayed out a long time."

"He done good that way."

"Yeah," Cleve said. "He done all right. Lasted a number of years." Red Yount said the coroner's verdict had been alcohol poisoning. Some balding, half-failed white physician had scribbled this on a death certificate, which would later be re-typed by some dreaming girl. "A number of years." Behind the wind's cold sound Cleve could sense the murmuring of the river below the cut sod bank just back of the house. Lately, since Lonnie'd left, he had been imagining the water's sound even when he wasn't hearing it. All his life he had gone to bed with that murmur, awakened with it, slept beneath it, lain sleepless listening to Lonnie's tubercular breath and the summer water. His father had built the four-room house in the spring and summer of 1947, when Cleve was two and Lonnie was on his way to being born. He'd built it with planks and nails bought the fall of 1945 with army mustering-out pay, warped planks and rusted nails by 1947. The building seemed to contain what they were in the way it looked: peeling, never repainted, standing alone above the river in the eddying yellow dust.

"So he got away from here," Red Yount said. "Anyway, that must have made him happy."

"Probably so."

"We'll get him home," the deputy said. "But you got to do something about having him buried."

"Give me a minute," Cleve said. "I want to get my coat and hook a ride with you" – which he knew was against the rules, probably illegal.

But the near-winter wind was burning from the clear and dry southern sky, and he figured Yount, who had been Indian Deputy since before Cleve was born, wouldn't refuse him. Yount had come home to this job, a decorated ex-Marine re-turning from Okinawa in 1945. "Ain't supposed to be giving any rides," the deputy said. "You duck down if we meet some-body. I'll leave you off before we get into town."

"I'll just be a minute," Cleve said. He was surprised when Yount followed him into the house. The coal-oil lantern on the table was flickering in the drafts. On a white muslin cloth next to the lamp lay the disassembled parts of a Remington 30-06 Cleve had been checking and oiling. He'd bought the rifle in a Klamath Falls hockshop and wanted to be sure everything was in working order, that nothing was worn and that none of the springs was loose. Around the walls hung his traps and two other rifles in scabbards. Piled in one corner was his saddle and horse gear.

"That money was what did it," the deputy said. "Never was right, giving people all that money."

Cleve dug for his coat in the pile of winter clothes behind the double bed where he slept alone.

"You get a deer?" the deputy asked.

"Yeah, I did." Cleve had killed thirteen deer, seven bucks and six does. He had sold the bucks to white hunters who had frozen at the moment of kill or had drunk through their sporting trip from Portland or Eugene or wherever it was. One of the butchered does was hanging now in the back bedroom. The others were in a locker in the Donan cold-storage plant. The room stank of leather and grease and dried blood, of hunting. "I got him hung in the back room," Cleve said. "I'm eating on him."

"You got him tagged?" the deputy asked. "You guys got the money now, you got to act like everybody else."

"Yeah, I got him tagged." Until the reservation had dissolved, the tribes hunted freely. Now they were bound by state regulations. Cleve had killed thirteen deer and hadn't bought a tag. The doe hanging in the back room was illegal.

"I guess maybe you did," the deputy said. "I remember somebody saying you bought a tag." He walked around the room slowly, looking at the gear. Cleve buttoned his blanket-lined Levi's jacket. The right sleeve was torn and the lining clotted with cheat-grass stickers. He'd worn it the winter before while feeding cattle. Lately he'd thought of buying a sheepskin-lined leather coat like the ones pictured in the slick-paper magazines on the stand in Prince's Tavern.

"You ready?" Cleve asked the deputy.

"I'm looking around. Let me look around." Dust was blowing past the Plymouth, and on the highway three empty cattle trucks went by, one right behind the other. Cleve wished the house was miles into the backwoods where the river would flow quietly and he wouldn't have to see anything but the water and tree shadows on the ripples, with porcupine and birds and maybe some deer. He hated the barbed wire and the railroad I-beam cattle guard and the Plymouth waiting for him in the dusty bowl before the house.

Red Yount was fingering the pieces of the 30-06 mechanism spread on the table. Cleve wished he had not asked the deputy for a ride into town. He hated it that the man was inside his house. He remembered the jail cell in the basement of the old town hall in Donan. "You're used to it," Red Yount had said, bringing him something to eat, a hamburger and glass of milk from the lunch counter in Prince's. "Ought to be like coming home." Cleve had been in for six months that time, the last time. Car theft. One drunk night in a deer hunter's Jeep station wagon. The deputy shoved the tray under the bars of the door. Cleve had been there three times before that, each time drunk and disorderly, but each time only for a week or ten days. Six months was different, sitting in the dampness and dim light, listening to mice and wasting out one of the summers of his life.

Cleve remembered listening for the whistle marking hours from the cupola atop the city hall, asking the deputy what day it was and Yount refusing to tell him, saying, "We'll let you know. Don't worry."

Cleve had never been back to jail. He never drank again. And he wasn't going back.

He wondered how to get Yount away from the illegal doe in the back room.

"Ain't no use hanging around here," Cleve said.

The deputy settled himself into the rocking chair and lit a filter cigarette. "I give up rolling 'em," he said, dropping his kitchen match on the floor. "Them roll-your-owns was killing my wind; they do that." Yount began telling about Lonnie. The Red Bluff city police found Lonnie passed out on the pedestrian walkway of the highway bridge over the Sacramento River, $3,147 in his wallet and stuffed into his various pockets when they took him in, alive but unconscious. "They could have pumped his stomach if they'd have knowed," the deputy said. "But you can't think of everything." They found the rest of the money, $27,292, in a box containing a never-worn pair of new Justin boots, the bills in a brown paper bag stuffed into one boot top. Yount ground his cigarette out under his heel. "Now," he said, getting to his feet. "Before we take off, you want to show me that carcass? I only want to look at the tag."

"No need," Cleve said. "I cut off the head. Buried it. Tag was with it."

"Maybe I'll just look at it anyway."

"Maybe you won't. Lonnie's dead. I better get to town. I better see about all that."

"I'm going to see that deer," Red Yount said. "Then you and me are going to town." He unsnapped the leather cover over his .38 pistol. "You don't make me any trouble now," the deputy said. "I don't want to have to take you in for resisting."

"Let's go," Cleve said. "Like we was friends. There won't be any trouble at all."

"But I ain't your friend. There's no way we're friends. Which door is that deer behind?"

"Why not forget it? Go off and leave and forget I ever asked for a ride."

"Just show me that animal." The deputy lifted his .38 from his holster and turned it in his hand. "I got to just take a look."

"Okay," Cleve said. "I'll show you." His voice sounded strange to him, and he moved quickly past the other man. As the deputy passed into the dark room where the carcass hung,

Cleve opened his skinning knife.

"Doe," the deputy said. "I knew damned well." He cocked the pistol and began to turn just as Cleve slipped the knife beneath the deputy's right ear. He twisted the knife and felt the hot splash of blood over his hand and arm.

Red Yount was on the floor, twitching beneath the carcass of the doe. Wondering if he should be sorry and knowing that he wasn't, hadn't been since the moment of killing, Cleve watched the deputy until he was sure it was over. Then Cleve put his knife away, washed his hands and went outside. He drove the Plymouth behind the house, where it couldn't be seen from the road.

Cleve walked toward Donan. It was almost evening when he started down the hill behind town, following a logger's skid trail, the blood already dry on his coat sleeve. Below, through the tops of the scrub pine, he could see the tinsheathed buildings, smoke trailing up from the brick chimney above the shop-built stove at the back of Decker and Preston's Garage. Cleve wondered how many of them were gathered there and if someone had gone across to Prince's for a case of beer and if they knew about Lonnie. Wind was blowing down the dusk-filled empty street as he stepped in the back door of the garage and saw three of them around the stove. Big Jimmy and his running pal, Clarence Dunes, and Lester, the mechanic. The only car inside was Big Jimmy's baby-blue convertible. An open case of Bud sat on the floor by the stove.

Cleve walked slowly to the row where they stood, turned his back to the stove and stood with them. Lester Braddock was older than the rest, around thirty-five, a small and bull-chested man wearing stiff new coveralls. He opened a beer for Cleve. "Drink that," he said. "They're looking for you, man. They found old Yount."

Cleve stood with the cold bottle in his hand. "I'll take off in a minute," he said. "I just want to say how I want Lonnie taken care of."

Cleve began to talk. A half mile below his house the river vanished underground. Cleve had dreamed of the river, and because of that dream, because Lonnie's death and the dream were all connected with the sound of water falling, he wanted to send Lonnie down through the boulders to the place where the water was sucked into the earth. The water fell between boulders in a long black lava rockslide to resurface at the bottom of the ridge, over a mile away, and the sound of the falling was hollow, as if the water dropped a great distance onto a plate of steel. He and Lonnie had played there as children. Their father had set up a system of net-holding wires among the boulders, and they had watched him scramble barefoot over the boulders, pulling trout from the nets, secured by a stranded rawhide riata he used for a safety line.

At the beginning of the war a child from some other family had fallen into the water and been sucked underground, the body never recovered; and on the flat-surfaced boulders near the water's edge a dim cross had been smeared with greenish house paint, covering more-ancient signs and drawings, memorializing that drowned, now-forgotten child. Cleve had dreamed of being that child, of falling and never being found. That's what he wanted for Lonnie.

Big Jimmy and Clarence Dunes stood looking at him. Lester was older and knew better. He wouldn't look at Cleve and Cleve was grateful. They'd all been friends, but Lester was the oldest and the only one who'd probably act like he had any sense of how it was to hear your brother was dead. Cleve finished the beer, drinking quickly in long gulps, and threw the can into an empty trash barrel. "Thanks," he said. Cleve looked at Lester, who was staring at the floor. "I'll see you around." He started to walk from the stove without any further idea of where he was going after the door that led outside, and Big Jimmy hooked him by the shoulder. Jimmy was tall, over six feet, and fat, his belly hanging down until only the bottom tip of his silver buckle could be seen. His face was like a full moon, always seeming placid and untroubled, even when

he was fighting. "They ain't going to go for that," he said.
"Some crazy idea like that, no way." He kept his hand on
Cleve's shoulder.

"You got to just steal him," Cleve said. He told them how
they should put Lonnie on a raft and send him down the river
at night. Jimmy dropped his hand and began to talk like *he* was
getting excited, like all he wanted was for somebody to tell him
it was possible, that they could make it work. He said, "We
could take a few bottles of whiskey and tell everybody. Everybody'll come." Cleve could never remember seeing Jimmy
even look excited before.

Not even when Lonnie burned the slaughterhouse. Coming
home from the All-Indian Rodeo in McDermit on the Fourth
of July 1961, their parents had burned while parked and sleeping alongside the gravel road south of Denio in a six-year-old
Chevrolet two-door. When the boys heard what had happened, Lonnie began a three-day drunk which ended only
when he opened the door and looked into the charred interior
and smelled the fecal stench of the automobile. That night he
carried a five-gallon can of kerosene to the slaughterhouse on
the upper edge of the reservation town of Donan and ignited
the buildings and hide pile. The next morning the odor of
burnt hair and cooking flesh had been mixed with the smoke of
blood-impregnated wood hanging in a gray haze. At daybreak
Lonnie returned to the house and found police waiting. "How
many things do you regret about your life?" The judge had
asked him that. "Everything," Lonnie had answered. "Like
you would, if you was anybody." Big Jimmy had sneered.
"Just drawed him more time," he'd said. "Don't make sense."
And now he seemed excited, now that it was too late. Cleve
saw Lonnie, the sterile white room, walls and floor of green
ceramic tile, rubber hoses curled and hung above faucets, the
body naked on a concrete slab; and the man writing quickly –
alcohol poisoning – then leaving the room.

It was decided then, and Cleve hid in the trunk of Jimmy's
baby-blue Buick convertible. They headed south, toward Red

Bluff. Cleve was curled on burlap sacks around a half-case of Olympia. Lester was driving because Jimmy said he was too stirred up. Cleve could feel each jar of the rough asphalt. At first, he tried to keep track of the curves, remembering the road, knowing where they were for the first fifteen minutes. Now he could only tell that they were moving fast. He'd finished three beers and started on another. He wondered a little about where they were going, but he really didn't care. Then the car swerved heavily, throwing him against Jimmy's spare tire, and he heard shouting from inside the car. He remembered the burned-out odor of his father's Chevrolet, imagined himself charred, his head filled with that stench, and then he was against the trunk lid and the car was going over.

His head hurt when the car stopped moving. He felt something running over the side of his face and wondered if it was blood or else beer. He saw spot lights through the crack of the gaping trunk lid. A man called, "Come out with your hands in the air, you bastards." He heard Jimmy wailing. The car was right side up. He heard Jimmy say, "Lester's hurt. Oh, God, I think Lester's dead." Cleve jumped down from the trunk of the car and began to run away from the lights, back down the road. He heard the *crack-crack* of shots and the whine of bullets passing. He dodged, tried to keep dodging like a coyote, then something lifted him up, and he fell skidding onto the asphalt and lay there exploring with his fingers the cool granular surface of the road, each embedded pebble a mountain he must climb; and for a moment it seemed the highway was a river he was flowing down. Jimmy was screaming – you killed him you *sonsabitches* – and Cleve knew he was killed and that the wind had stopped and that he was going down and down the river with Lonnie toward the place where they were capable of infinite resistance.

We Are Not in This Together

THIS TIME it was a girl Halverson knew, halfway eaten and her hair chewed off. She had been awake in the night; she'd been afraid and whimpering as the great bear nudged at the side of the nylon tent like a rooting hog. She held to the other girl's hand, and began to scream only when the long claws ripped her out of her sleeping bag, continuing to scream as she was being dragged away, the feathery down from the sleeping bag floating above the glowing coals of a pine-knot fire. This time it was someone he knew; and he lay still in the darkness and the warmth of his own bed and tried to understand the feeling of knowing you were killed before you were dead.

Thinking was beyond the point. The last time Halverson lay awake like this, the first weekend the hard wind-drifted snow was plowed off the Going-to-the-Sun Highway over Logan Pass, it had been a fetus – not a fetus really, a child, stillborn, a baby girl dropped in a roadside trash container at the east end of Two Medicine Lake and found by workmen. A dead baby wrapped in a pink motel towel and thrown into a garbage can. It could not have been anything like indifference which brought someone to such a burial. More like the need to get rid of what can happen. Walk into the wind and your eyes will water.

But in the beginning there was Darby, and the way Halverson saw her avoiding mirrors. There was no explaining it to Darby, but early in May, when the aspen leaves along the middle fork of the Flathead were lime green and just emerging, Halverson began to think he saw what Darby was seeing when she quickly looked away from the long mirror she'd hung in his bedroom. Halverson would glance up on the evenings when she was home, and see Darby with her stockinged feet up on the hearth before the fire, intent on one of her magazines – the old issues of the *National Geographic* she brought with her when she came to live with him – and he would see her as she would look when she was old. Her eyeglasses would be thicker and distorting her eyes until they were strange as the eyes of owls; eventually, he knew, she would be fumbling and blind. Her hands would touch at things she could not see, tentative and exploring. If he stayed with her long enough there would be the time when she fell, the cracking of bone, a sound he imagined as he watched her turn the magazine pages; and some indeterminate time after that, he would be alone and old, his hands touching and exploring each thing in this familiar room as he talked to some memory of his father about sharpening a knife or the color of hatchery trout.

Halverson told Darby that he would never have children if he had anything to say about it. He told her that he could not go on living with her, and that he would not ever try living with another woman. He told her they were better off alone.

"I'm sorry," he told her, expecting her to argue. But she only looked back to her magazine.

"No," she said. "It's not that."

The next night, when he came home from hauling cedar logs, his cabin was filled with chairs and tables made of twisted and shellacked bamboo. Bright patterns of lavender and orange tropical flowers were splashed across the cushions. His old furniture was piled out in the pole barn where he sheltered the truck in winter. "Don't you think about worrying," Darby said. "This is all in my name. I'm making the payments. Fifty-seven dollars a month." There was a new canvas drop cloth over the chair on his side of the fireplace, so the fabric would stay clean.

"While I pay for every bite there is to eat," Halverson said. There had been nothing kind he could say.

"I always wanted this," Darby said. "It's like the South Pacific, don't you think?"

"Pretty close," Halverson said. He didn't mention the notion of her leaving again.

That which is not useful is vicious: in needlepoint, those words had been framed on his grandfather's wall, attributed to Cotton Mather. Halverson's father burned the plaque along with the bedding heaped on the bed where his grandfather had shivered away his last months. The blankets smelled of camphor as they burned. Halverson's grandfather had died angry, refusing to eat and starving himself. His father had never helped his mother try to make the old man eat, but had sat in the kitchen glaring at the snowfall outside the window over the sink while the persuading went on. Halverson had been six or seven, but he could still hear his mother's voice murmuring from the old man's room at the back of the house.

"There is only so much sin for each of us," his mother had repeated over and over. Halverson had never thought of it much until now, but he knew the old man had not been sinning.

In the bedroom, the digital clock atop Halverson's Sony TV showed the time to be 12:52. The pint of Jack Daniel's was empty and Halverson was nowhere near sleep. He always tried to be sleeping when Darby came home late from her bartending shift. He didn't want to hear who had gone off with the wrong partner at closing time, or which children slept in the car while their parents drank and quarreled after the drive-in movie.

But tonight there was the girl; she was young, and now she was dead, the round slope of her tight belly eaten away by the grizzly. Her hair, which hung down her back in a tangled red-tinted rope, had been gnawed off her skull. Park rangers were searching with rifles. Halverson got up and went into the bathroom and turned the shower to steaming hot, then down to cold while he stood under the spray, trying not to gasp or flinch. He shaved for the second time that day, and then pulled a flannel shirt from his closet, turned the cuffs up, and dragged on his work pants and laced his boots. His face was smooth and slick as he rubbed at his eyes, thinking: just this one time, just tonight, another drink.

The girl who died had worked in the bar where Darby worked. Halverson stopped there each evening for his pint of Jack Daniels and a glass or two of beer. He'd joked with the girl only a few nights ago about how she was going to be stuck in this country if she stayed much longer. "Five years ... you can't help going native." It had been something to say while she rang up the pint. She was a dark and not exceptionally pretty girl who had come west from a rich suburb of Columbus, Ohio. She had quit the Wildlife Biology School down in Missoula and come to Columbia Falls with a boy who sold cocaine to the skiers in Whitefish and spent his summers climbing mountains. Halverson wondered what happened to you with cocaine. When the boy was caught and sentenced to five years in the state prison at Deer Lodge, maybe three years with probation, she took the barmaid job and said she was going to wait. According to Darby, she had been; there hadn't been any fooling around.

Halverson drove down the canyon from his cabin toward the neon thickness of light over Columbia Falls. Outside the tavern he parked and listened to the soft racketing of the tappets in his Land Rover.

Halverson sat watching the beer signs flicker on and off, and then he drove home. Below the cabin, he parked the Land Rover beside the shadowy bulk of his 350 Kenworth diesel log-hauling truck. Halverson spent his working days drifting the truck down the narrow asphalt alongside the Flathead River, hauling cedar logs to the shake mill below Hungry Horse. The amber-hearted cedar smelled like medicine ought to smell. The work was like a privilege, mostly asphalt under the tires and those logs. And now he was quitting.

Halverson climbed up and sat in the Kenworth, snapped on the headlights so they shone into the scrub brush at the edge of the timber. He was not going out the next morning. The truck was ready, log bunks chained down for the trip into the mountains before sunrise, but he was not going to work come morning.

He was imagining the bear. The dished face of the great animal would rear up simple and inquisitive from vines where serviceberries hung thick as wine grapes. The dark nose would be a target under the cross hairs. The sound of the shot would reverberate between the mineral-striped walls of the cirque, where the glaciers had spent their centuries eating away rock. Far away a stone would be dislodged and come rattling down over the slide. The square-headed peaks would dampen the sound to silence.

Halverson could hear the stone clattering on other stones after the echo of the shot diminished to nothing. But he could not imagine the animal falling. He couldn't imagine anything beyond that first shot. Halverson shut off the headlights on the Kenworth and went into the cabin and punched off the alarm, and was satisfied to sleep.

The girl had died two nights ago in the backcountry of Glacier Park. With another girl, she'd camped at the distant eastern end of Quartz Lake in the Livingston Range. Here there were no trails cut through the deadfall lodgepole along the shore, the section of the park kept closest to true wilderness, miles from other campers. It was territory Halverson knew, from those late summer encampments his father had called vacations. All his working life Halverson's father had drawn wages from the park: trail crew supervisor in the summer and snow clearance in the winter; feeding baled hay to the elk and deer during the really bad winters. Each September after the Labor Day tourists had gone home, his father took time to camp in the backcountry, to hide out, as he said, and let his whiskers grow and learn to smell himself again. You go and forget who you are, his father said, when you never get wind of yourself. The time that don't count, his father liked to say, meaning a thing John Muir said about wandering the mountains: *the time that will not be subtracted from the sum of your life.* But something had been subtracted. His father died of a heart seizure, defibrillation the doctors called it, when he was thirty-nine years old. There was a winter morning when Halverson's mother stood in the lighted bedroom doorway, saying to Halverson, "Don't you come in here!" Then there was the door closing, and her shrieking. *You don't come in here!* After a while she was quiet. And then she came out of the bedroom and closed the door and washed her face. Then she turned to Halverson and said, *he is dead.*

Halverson was forty-two now, three years older than his father had been when he died. He had not been in the park, except to shortcut through, since the funeral. What year could that have been?

The girl who survived told of awakening to hear the bear grunting outside the tent, and the other girl whimpering. What I thought, the girl said, is *thank God it is out there.* That was all I could think, like I knew there was a bear outside, but it was *outside,* you see. The girl who survived told how she and the other girl held hands, and tried to stay quiet. Then the nylon tent ripping away, and the vast dark animal dragging the other girl from her sleeping bag; and the beginning of the screaming, really just long breathless shrieking as the bear killed her. That was the way she told it, the girl who survived; *he just dragged her away and killed her.* After a while, the girl said, I climbed a tree. The insides of her thighs were torn by the bark. But it didn't make any difference, the girl said, he didn't come for me, he didn't want me.

The girl spent most of the next day making her way out along the six-mile rocky shoreline of Quartz Lake, back toward the trails and other hikers. Before nightfall the hunt began. Rangers with rifles dropped at the shore of the lake from helicopters and discovered the half-eaten body. Halverson burned the newspaper in his fireplace, and looked around at Darby's flowered furniture, remembering her notion of making a getaway to some Pacific island. "Marlon Brando did it," Darby said.

"Three or four days," Halverson told Darby. "You do some bowling or something." He didn't tell her he was heading out of Montana, over to Spokane where nobody would know him, to buy a rifle.

"Which one is it?"

"Nobody," he said. "I wouldn't be chasing a woman."

Halverson spent two days talking to gun men in the surplus houses and sporting goods stores, and ended up spending $440. for a falling block Ruger #1, fitted out with a Redfield 3 x 9 variable wide-angle scope, and firing a .458 Winchester magnum bullet. One reasonably placed shot would kill anything native to North America, really anything anywhere, the salesman said, except for maybe a whale. Except for maybe a blue whale, and there were not many of them left. The salesman laughed, but then shook his head like there was nothing funny about dead whales.

The walnut stock swung hard and secure against Halverson's shoulder, and the mechanism worked with heavy, poised delicacy. The series of simple firing motions could be performed in two or three seconds, which was important, because the grizzly is as fast as a thoroughbred horse: three hundred yards in twenty seconds on level ground. But the rifle was extravagantly accurate at distance. Breathe, hold, and fire with the soft draw of the fingertip; and the animal would be dead. There should be no need for speed.

Late the second afternoon, Halverson drove to a gun club north of Spokane, beyond the industrial park around the Kaiser aluminum plant. At the gun club he fired nine rounds at range targets, three more for pleasure. The pattern of the last three rounds, at two hundred yards, was smaller than the spread of his fingers: all into the back of the throat, inside past the carnivorous fangs and into the soft and vulnerable flesh above the dark palate. Halverson could see the leafy boughs with their clusters of red and purple berries whipping after the animal fell, and then quiet in the noontime heat. When he finished firing, his shoulder ached like it had been struck a dozen times with a heavy mallet. The next day he outfitted himself with a light, down-filled sleeping bag and a one-man sleeve tent, a lightweight butane GAZ stove that nested with cooking pots, a spoon and fork and an elaborate Swiss Army knife, and a Buck skinning knife, packets of freeze-dried food in heavy aluminum foil, and detailed hikers' maps of Glacier Park. He knew the park well enough, but the maps, with their shaded precision, were like verification of his accuracy. The bill for the heavy-duty backpack and the traveling gear was almost as much as he'd paid for the rifle, but that was fine with him. Halverson had worked twenty-three years to earn a paid-off Kenworth, and now his time had come and he could just write checks. The gear would start with him, new and clean, and would wear and stain and become his in the wilderness.

Darby was awake. Just out of the shower and blow-drying her hair at the kitchen table while she sipped instant coffee. Halverson had driven back from Spokane in the early morning hours. Now he stood in the doorway with the rifle in his hands. Darby nodded her head, as if acknowledging some premonition. "Who on earth," she said, "can you think you are making plans for?" She was staring at the rifle, the hair-dryer aimed at the ceiling. "Why in the world?" As if this could be his way of making up for her flowered furniture.

So Halverson told her. Just killing one bear, for a head, to mount on the wall, to get things even. Anyway, he said, I never killed one. I am owed one. And no, he told her, she could not come along.

"The rangers killed one," she said. "An old one, a cripple."

Halverson told her it wasn't enough.

"I'm going," Darby said. "I'm going and you can't stop me. I'll just follow."

"Why in the hell?" Halverson said. "This is not any of your concern." No, he told her, she was not going.

"So half the head will be mine," she said.

Halverson mimicked her voice. "What about me?" he said.

"How about mine?" He told her she would never make it.

"I got boots," Darby said. "I walk more on a night shift than you walk in three weeks. You better worry about yourself. Back and forth on them duckboards behind that bar is more than you ever think about walking. What you should do is get in some running. Before the moon comes back, you should get in better shape than you are. I can carry extra food, think of that, and you could quit shaving." The hair-dryer looked like a thick-barreled weapon as she shook it while she talked; and the silence after she shut off its whirring let Halverson see how loud their voices had been. There had been the years of climbing through the brush, setting three-quarter-inch cable choker behind the D8 skid Cats when he was breaking in; and then more years bucking a chain saw up those mountains and falling timber, all those years until he had the money for the down payment on the Kenworth, and he was hard as he would ever need to be. Halverson thought of telling her about how many years he had worked to be in shape for this, but after she shut off the hair-dryer, he didn't say a thing. He kept quiet.

"You come out here." Halverson crossed the kitchen and stood at the open back door, fishing in his coat pocket for a cartridge, and then slipping the round into the firing chamber. "You shoot this thing and see. You just see." Darby followed him barefoot out into the weedy lot where he showed her how to hold the rifle, her hands small and white against the stained walnut stock. She almost couldn't reach the trigger.

"Where?"

"Anywhere."

Halverson was surprised by how quick she fired, the roar as she cast a shot toward the timbered hillside. She stepped backward from the recoil. But only for a moment, crouched and regaining her balance, did she look bewildered.

"You should know something," she said. "You are not the first one to try that trick. I been mixed with before by you wise-assed boys." She grinned like a child in the morning sunlight.

"Have it the way you like."

For three weeks, while they waited on the full moon, Halverson kept on driving his truck while Darby went on pulling her bartending shift. He gave up on the Jack Daniel's and slept anyway. He lost weight and quit smoking, and felt he was becoming less than himself.

They crossed at Polebridge over the North Fork of the Flathead River almost at midnight, under a full moon as they'd planned, carrying enough food for several weeks; the freeze-dried stuff in aluminum packets, a half pound of salt, a brick of cheese; potatoes and onions to fry with the fish he'd catch; and even a heavy uncut side of bacon, Darby's idea. Halverson wanted to travel light. But there was no arguing. "We can camp and you can travel out. We are not going to be moving around. We will make a place." She was carrying her share, and she bought her own gear, every few days bringing home something new to show him: a frameless pack, a Dacron insulated sleeping bag she claimed would dry better than his goose feathers, an expensive breakdown fly rod. She would smile and fondle each thing, as if this was all part of her plan to move away across the Pacific Ocean. As a last gesture, she trimmed his beard. Halverson wanted to shave it off after the first week, because of the itching, and because the gray in it surprised him. "You leave it grow," she said. "It makes you look like a movie star." After the second week the itching stopped and Halverson got used to it and stopped leaning out to see himself in the huge rectangular mirrors hung on either side of the truck cab. What Darby said was true; he looked like some visitor who might be in town for only a night or so.

The walking was easy in the moonlight, along the twisting roadway past the ranger station at the lower end of Bowman Lake and then on the wide park service trail over Cerulean Ridge toward Quartz Lake, stepping in and out of the shadows of moonlight. Presently, the early midsummer sun rose in a great blossom over the cirque wall beyond Quartz Lake, near the blunt peak Halverson figured from the map had to be Redhorn, light coming down at them and the shadows receding

like tide. Halverson felt as if he could be walking into his childhood where he might find the strange thin-armed boy in his
mother's box camera photographs, himself at thirteen, sol-
emnly holding aloft a small trout; the person he had been, real
and turning over stones in a creek, searching for caddis fly
larvae, or in a hot meadow catching grasshoppers with his hat.
The boy would pay him no attention, intent on catching bait,
wearing no shirt under raggedy bib overalls. A boy who existed only in tones of photographic gray.

They got themselves off the trail before there was a chance
of meeting other hikers, and made a cold camp. As they wove
out through the open brush, Halverson deliberately stepped
on the clustering mushrooms, like he was balancing rock to
rock across a stream; and as he slept in the afternoon stillness,
he dreamed of the mushrooms crackling under his boots. They
looked poisonous, wide caps sprinkled with virulent red. Over
twenty years since he had been inside this park, and now, bad
dreams.

The next night they worked past the camps at the lower end
of Quartz Lake, tents and the sparking remains of a fire, the
end of any sort of trail. They made maybe five or six hundred
yards up the north side of the lake, even with moonlight coming bright over the water, stepping along in the shallows, in
and out of shadows cast by the timber, afraid their splashing
would be heard by the campers down the shore where the fire
still glowed. In a grassy opening between deadfalls they laid
their packs against a log, and Darby unbuttoned her shirt and
dropped it and stood naked to the waist. "You better get on
some dry socks," Halverson said.

"I never did this before," Darby said. "I never stood like this
in the moon before."

Halverson looked away. "Now is not the time for these
things. You just worry about changing your socks." While he
lay listening to her breathe in her sleep and watched the stars
make their slow way around the moon, Halverson reflected on
how long it had been since he and Darby had been after one
another. The first night when he went into the tavern and she

was there, tending the bar, Halverson drank late, rolling dice in a long game of Ship, Captain, and Crew; and toward closing time she looked at him and said, fine, all right she would, after she counted out the till, when he asked her if she had ever gone riding in a logging truck. Even though she invited herself into his bed after she found out he owned the truck and cabin, what they got from each other was not founded on any financial considerations; she kept her job and nobody was bought or sold. But now they were stopped, these months since spring; and maybe the way they slept without touching was causing the changes in her, thin white hands lifting her breasts in the moonlight, if she was changing and hadn't always been ready for anything, secretly. Darby was from a town named Wasco, in the great central valley of California; and her breasts were lined faintly by stretch marks. There had been other men and probably children. He wondered how much she told him, and why they could live together and not tell each other what was true.

After sunrise, picking their way along where that lone surviving girl had fought her way back toward the world, Halverson followed Darby and wished there could be some sign of that girl, a rip of cloth he could lift off a snag and tuck into his breast pocket as a sign of his intentions. But there was no hurry, and they went slowly, heading up to the swampy creek-water flat between Quartz and Cerulean Lakes, willow ground, and thick with ferns and berry brush where the bear would come to feed. Up there he would be deep below the rough high circle of hanging wall peaks, looking up to those spoon-shaped cirques carved by the ancient glaciers to the remnants of ice which would show faint white under the moon on these clear nights, and into the country where his business waited. There was no hurry and this walk was more and more a trip back into someone he had been. In the afternoon Halverson surprised himself as they stood resting on a rocky point overlooking the lake – he put his arm around Darby and held her to his side. She smelled of a deep sour odor, but it was not entirely unpleasant; it was as if all the stench from the barroom was seeping out of her. Most importantly, he was trying to figure just when he had stood in this very place before. The complex green and yellow etching of lichen on the rocks was familiar. What if you could recall even the look of the clouds from every moment of your life? There was too much of himself he was bringing along, so much he felt dizzy holding onto Darby; and he shut his mind against it.

The third night they camped a quarter mile up from Quartz Lake, toward Cerulean, north of the swampy willow ground in an open grove of stunted black cottonwood on a little knoll. The fire, their first fire, was in the ashes of another fire – where those girls might have built their fire. The beaver trappers had come into this country close to 150 years ago, when there was no one else in this high country, to this place which had no history except for the Blackfeet. But the beaver trapping must have been poor, because beaver never lived above timberline where the little creeks froze to the bottom in winter, except for the deep holes where the trout survived. There had never been enough beaver to draw the trappers. Maybe the only past here was the one he brought, him and Darby, what they remembered.

They were alone finally, up toward the head of the fifteen or so mile-long valley through the ancient glacier had eroded and left for the lakes, more than 2,000 feet below the ring of peaks which had shown east of them like a crown when touched by the last sunlight. Darby was frying four small cutthroat caught from the ripple where the creek slipped into Quartz Lake when a loon called, its mournful laugh echoing over and back into the settling coolness under the mountains before moonrise, a sound Halverson had not heard since one of the far places of his childhood, but perfectly known and expected, not surprising as it came back off the shadowed walls above them. As the moon turned through the sky those shadows moved as if the mountains were going to fall out over the fire and the creek water below.

"What were they doing here?" Darby asked.

"Who?"

"Those children." Halverson was astonished when she turned from the fire; there were tears in her eyes, lighted by the flames. "If what I'm thinking about is any of your business," she said, and she rubbed at her face and went to turn her sleeping bag open.

In the morning, Halverson set up a business of camp tending meant to last. Where they could listen to the water of the creek falling through a raft of deadwood as they perched themselves each morning after coffee, he picked a fallen barkless lodgepole to serve as toilet seat, and spooled a roll of yellow paper on a dead branch like a flag. In the afternoon he shot and butchered a yearling mule deer and ran the meat high in a tree, out of the reach of any bear, the carcass wrapped in cheesecloth to keep away the flies. In the gray light after sunset the dead animal in that white wrap of cloth turned slowly on the rope. "They ain't going to get to it," Halverson said. "But they will be coming to see."

"The bears and squirrels," Darby said. "And the park rangers. You are going to draw a crowd."

"Everybody who is interested," Halverson said. The intestines from the slaughtered yearling had been warm and slippery, and the odor of the kill had been acrid in the late afternoon warmth. Halverson smiled for the first time, smelling his hands, where the faint odor of deer remained.

How long had he refused returning into these mountains? Why had that girl come here from that rich place on the outskirts of Columbus, Ohio? Why come hunting a place where there is no one else? The girl had used the excuse of school for getting away from whatever crowded life she had been born to, then quit her wildlife biology studies down in Missoula and gone off to Columbia Falls with that boy who delivered cocaine and climbed in the summer, and now she was dead in these mountains.

"What do you guess she was up to?" Halverson said.

"You wait and you wait," Darby said, "and everything takes all the time it can. Then it all comes in a hurry." She shook salt over the venison steaks in the frying pan. "You . . ." she said and waited. "Why don't you ever fuck me?"

"Why are you talking like shit?" Halverson said. "You tell me what fucking has to do with this?"

"Nothing. I'm just wondering. She never talked anything serious to me, like I never knew anything, or come from anywhere, and all the time I could have told her."

"You could have told her what?"

"About how we go looking for some one thing to be, and there's nothing to find."

The biggest trouble, he understood, was that he was not afraid. Halverson tried to center himself into that frail girl, the girl who died, and then he shook his head. He wished he had brought a pint of whiskey so that this single night, when everything was ready, he could rest here with his common sense turning circles and be inside that girl and feeling the warmth from this fire and the cool night on her back, drifting in someone else – a rich girl estranged from the rich part of Ohio – and no rifle.

Maybe that would have worked – no rifle. At least he might have been a little bit afraid and not sitting here with thoughts of his dead father, and his mother living her life out in San Diego. His mother in a wicker chair on the front lawn and sunset over the warships in San Diego harbor; Halverson saw her, and some dim memory of his father kneeling in the snow to fasten the straps on her snowshoes, a logging road and larch in the background.

"Why don't you ever?" Darby said.

"What?"

"You know."

"Because you talk like you do."

Picking along the edge where the lodgepole timber leveled into the swamp, scouting the new territory, Halverson was walking alone when the old she-bear reared herself out of thick brush only a hundred or so yards before him. Listening but no doubt unable to make him out with her weak eyes, she was maybe ready to come at him and find out what he was, but more likely to drop and lope away. Halverson heard her snuffling; and as he had planned, but before he was able to understand this was not what he wanted, not this easiness, he centered the cross hairs just beneath her dark uplifted nose and fired. As he slipped his finger across the trigger, he was astonished by the noise, which hadn't mattered when he'd killed the doe, the hard jolt of the rifle stock against his shoulder and the crack that went echoing, the massive head jerking away, gone from the scope. Halverson thought he had missed, levered in another shell, thinking *nowhere*, then lifted his eye from the scope to see the bear floundering backward and sideways into the leafy brush, and falling as he had imagined. With such thoughtless luck he was done with it now, and had killed his grizzly, too quickly for recall, except for the diminishing echo of the rifle shot; and he was already sorry, knowing this one was wasted. There had to be another, stalked and properly confronted and then killed. There had to be time for thinking, and time for the bear, for hoping the animal might dimly sense the thing happening.

Halverson waited, listening, expecting Darby, who did not come, hearing nothing but the buzz of insects. Soon the birds began moving and calling in the trees once more, and then he went to the bear. The odor was rancid, and Halverson was surprised by the smallness of the dead animal, the raggedness of her coat, because already he could see it was a she-bear, an old one who looked to be shedding in mid-summer, the gray-tipped pelt ragged and almost slick to the hide around the rear haunches. An old one. The wrong one. The .458 magnum slug had entered her mouth and blown away the back of her skull. Halverson cupped his fingers into the wound and there was nothing to be felt but pulpy flesh and sharp bone fragments and warm blood, like thick soup.

He tasted the salty blood.

Kneeling beside the carcass, Halverson tried again to think of the dead girl in these mountains. The stench of the animal beside him was like a part of the air. Off in the willows a frog was croaking; and then he heard the first sounds of the helicopter, rotor blades cutting at the stillness as the aircraft came up along the length of Quartz Lake, the thunking louder until the helicopter hung between walls of the stippled rock face above him.

Downstream that roll of yellow toilet paper was spooled onto the dead branch like a flag. The helicopter turned and lifted, moved a half mile away. Halverson brought the rifle to his shoulder and through the eye of the scope watched the two men up there searching for him with binoculars. Don't find me, Halverson thought. This is none of your business, and it is not finished. We are not in this together.

It had to have been the echoing of the shot that drew the men in the helicopter. The afternoon of the day before he'd killed the yearling mule deer; and now, another shot, echoing down the length of the lake, they were after him. Only when the helicopter lifted and turned in three wide fluttering circles, and then bore off down the lake, going away, did Halverson pay attention to what came next. He would have to build a silencer.

Darby would not leave. "You got me here," she said, "so you are going to have trouble getting me out, even if they come looking." She was talking about the park service rangers. "There won't be the rifle, so there is nothing against the law with me being here." The carcass of the gutted doe was hanging a quarter-mile away, wrapped in cheesecloth. Halverson thought of that, but didn't say anything. Let her learn, if this is what she wants. Halverson went out of the park the next morning, carrying only the rifle, and drove back to his cabin in the canyon above Columbia Falls. Even without the pack it was a hard daylong march. Darby would be all right, or else she wouldn't. She had insisted on coming along, and she was into it.

The silencer turned out to be a reasonably simple piece of business. Halverson slipped an eight-inch section of the heavy plastic hot water tubing over thick rubber washers on the end of the rifle barrel; and when it was securely in place, he cut pipe threads on the outside of the tubing. This was a mount for the silencer. The thing itself consisted of two cylinders, a small perforated core of metal tubing inside a larger section of steel pipe, the space between them packed with sound-absorbing steel wool. Halverson brazed it together in the pole-walled shed back of his cabin, where he kept the Kenworth in winter, then screwed the silencer onto the threaded plastic pipe fixed to the end of the rifle barrel. It was like a small metal can hanging out there. He fired the rifle into the hillside back of the cabin, and the contraption worked. There was the crack of the magnum slug passing the sound barrier, he lost none of his muzzle velocity, but the explosive roar was absorbed in the steel wool. He was ready again. This time he would hunt quietly, secretly, and choose and get this properly done with. He called and had the telephone shut off, and the power, and the newspaper. Through it all he felt as if he were acting on precise instructions for going away that he did not need to understand. That night he thought of Darby up there alone in her sleeping bag, the frogs croaking in the darkness. He wondered if she was frightened, or if she was walking around naked amid the trees. If she touched herself in the night, who would she be thinking about? Before driving back to the park in the morning, he went into Columbia Falls and bought a newspaper to read with breakfast; and again acting on what seemed to be directives for survival somewhere else, a guidebook to edible species of mushrooms.

Darby had moved the camp. She found another fire ring a couple of miles upstream from their first camp, and said the ashes were fresh and no doubt it was the place where the girls had camped. "It was the right place, being here where they were," she said. Halverson had found her late in the afternoon, and now it was dark.

"Which one will you be?" Darby said. "One night you can be one, and I'll be the other, and then we can switch around. We can see which one gets eaten worst." She smiled as though this lewdness was very funny, and turned back to her work, frying three trout. "Maybe this is the place. When I was here alone, I tried to think what that girl was thinking, and it felt like the place."

"What did she think?"

But Darby didn't answer, and Halverson took the whiskey from his day-pack. Along with the book on mushrooms, he had brought a quart of Jack Daniel's. The firelight shone through the liquid like a dim lantern. "There was a man here, really a boy, the second night you were gone," Darby said. "One of those park service boys, just last year out of college in Vermont. He was looking for you. At least he was looking for someone with a rifle. He was frightened. That's what he said. Probably some lunatic son of a bitch, is what he said. I didn't say anything. I don't think he wanted to find anybody, least of all a man." She salted the frying fish. "He talked about how this park is open ground for crazies. What he said is lunatics. He said there was no control, and lunatics clustered in places where there was no control."

"Maybe he got it right. We might stay here forever. All the goddamned helicopters do no good. We might stay right here," Halverson said. "You know what I did? You guess ... I got back and there was a week's newspapers all over the porch." He was going to lie, there had been the newspapers, but the rest of this was going to be a lie. "I didn't call them and have the newspaper shut off, or the power company shut off the lights, or the telephone. Those things are going on back there, without us, to remind them. I could have shut it off, but I didn't." Halverson waited for her to look away from the fire and back toward him.

"Who are they reminding?" Darby said. "About what?"

When Halverson didn't answer, she went on. "What I did is, I slept with that boy. In his sleeping bag and mine zipped together. He was frightened and I felt like his mother, holding to him all night." Darby finally turned and looked at Halverson. "It was the right thing to do," she said.

"Did you fuck him?"

She nodded. She did not seem disturbed. "It was the right thing to do. I wanted to be with somebody, and it made him feel better."

Halverson was not frightened, and he was not angry. Maybe she did do the right thing, for her. It was not anything he could get himself to think about. "I guess we could have a drink together," Halverson said. Maybe each thing they were doing was the right thing to do. He poured them each a shot in the steel Sierra Club cups, and didn't say anything about how he was going to sit drunk in the night and see if he could see what it could maybe feel like to be that girl as the bear began nudging at the tent walls. He would get drunk and think he was alone and begin whimpering; and when he woke up and the hangover was gone, he would begin hunting.

Late in the night, sipping at his whiskey and sharpening his skinning knife by firelight, Halverson surprised himself. Darby was curled in her sleeping bag, maybe sleeping and maybe not, when Halverson for the first time in all this surprised himself absolutely by drawing the knife along the tender flesh inside his left forearm, careful to avoid the veins as they stood out, just softly tracing and watching the painless slide of the blade and the immediate welling streak of blood, holding himself so he did not force the blade deeper, pulling away just as he reached the wrist. After a moment of watching the blood gather and begin to drip, he held the knife low over the coals until the cutting edge began to glow red, and then breathing through his teeth, he seared the wound. The next morning, when Darby asked, he told her it had only been a test.

"Just practicing, I thought about cutting off a finger," he

said, which was a lie, "but then I thought, there is nothing to grieve over, so I didn't cut off no finger."

"That's fine," Darby said.

"The first blood," Halverson said, "was always mine."

"Never in the world," Darby said. "That story I told, about fucking with that boy, was a lie. I've had plenty of that. It didn't happen."

What Halverson did not tell her was that the whiskey worked: he finally dreamed of the girl who died. At least it was a dream he had never witnessed before, and it must have come from someone nearby. It must have been waiting. Below in some street there was the snow melting as it fell on wet black asphalt that flared under the headlights of a red Olds convertible which was backing out of a long driveway. In the street, the convertible did not move. The motor stopped and the headlights dimmed, and Halverson, in his sleep, thought: which window is this I am watching from?

Then he was awake and the fire was burned down to embers; and he listened to the snapping of pitch and Darby's breathing, and heard the rasping of brush against brush and stillness; and knew it was the girl's dream he was in because for the first time he was afraid. The rifle was there, he could touch it by reaching out, but he was trembling.

Another sound, and he lay there, not calling out to Darby because this was not her business, feeling his forearms tremble as a pine limb flared, and waiting for the rooting hoglike sound which never came. There was a whisper of air high in the yellow pine. The moon was gone. Off east the high wall of the cirque hung in delicate outline against the fainter blue of what had to be the sky turning toward morning. Nothing had happened, and as the dream began to fade there was nothing to do but rebuild the fire.

After breakfast, as she watched him scrubbing their plates with sand in the cold water at the edge of the stream, Darby got started talking about what was fair. She wanted seriously to try the rifle, not just firing off at nothing on a hillside, but killing. "You slice at your arm like that, you might cut your throat. Where would I be, when there was trouble?"

"What would you kill?"

Darby didn't answer, but turned her back to Halverson, unbuttoned her wrinkled blue work shirt and dropped it off her shoulders and sat facing the morning sun on a grassy ledge above the creek, slumping, as from the weight of her breasts. "No wonder you draw crowds," Halverson said, "sitting around bare-assed like that."

"Maybe I already did. Maybe I had a boatload of cowboys, and there is more coming in tonight, and maybe I am just warning you." The stretch marks on her breasts and over her hips were a silvery network in the light. So I was never pretty, she said, after their first night together, talking about the marks, tracing them with a fingertip after she turned on a light, showing them to him like some wound, but never explaining. I never been pretty because of these, she said, and he never asked where they came from.

"You are going to sunburn your tits," Halverson said, and he went off to the half-rotten cored-out deadfall where he kept the rifle hidden. Quietly he slipped a cartridge into the firing chamber and raised the rifle and fired without aiming, as she had that morning behind the cabin, only he was firing toward the grayish snowpack in the ravines on Redhorn Peak.

"I heard you," she said when he came back to where she sat in the sun. Halverson was carrying the rifle and her shirt was on and unbuttoned. "You missed," she said, and she looked around and bit at the tip of her index finger as she watched him eject the empty casing. Halverson put in another shell.

"Not now," she said. "I changed my mind."

There were no clouds anywhere in the long sky reaching off south and west from the peaks; and far off in the trough to the west, Quartz Lake shone under the late afternoon sun. Early that morning, standing over the darkness of Cerulean Lake,

Halverson had looked down from the logjam at the creek out-
let to trees floating upright far below the surface, his face mir-
rored among them, then spent the morning climbing along the
southern rise of the drainage. He was resting in the noontime
warmth on a rotting log, listening to the silence which whispered of insects, when he heard the dry cracking of a limb
breaking. A fragile dead branch stepped on and snapped, that
sound, from back the way he had come before breaking out
onto this open burn-slope.

But this was Darby, not a bear. She had followed him all this
way. Halverson watched as she came from the timber into the
sunlight maybe 150 yards down-slope, stopped and looked
around and didn't see him. Halverson watched as she undid
the buttons on her blue work shirt again, took it off and knotted the sleeves around her waist. This time she was wearing the
orange top to her swimming suit over her breasts. Watching
her through the scope on the rifle, the magnification bringing
her up to only fifteen or so yards, Halverson was surprised
how tanned she was from this last couple of weeks lying naked
in the afternoons while he was off hunting. There it was, this
other person she had become. What was she following, all this
way into his idea of what he had to do?

It was Darby, after he whistled softly to her and waved, who
first saw the bear. She sat beside him on the rotting log, not
saying anything, as if there was no reason to explain why she
spent this long day trailing him, and then she said, "Do you see
him?"

"Who?"

"Down over there."

There it was, down the length of her pointing arm, the bear
thrashing lazily in the berry brush, head down and only the
dark hump flashing at them occasionally. Halverson watched
through the scope, and saw the animal roll a great rotting log
for the grubs on the underside, the casual movement of enor-
mous strength like that of a man moving driftwood on a beach.

This sunny quiet day. Halverson wondered what he should do now, which move to make. Rest the rifle solidly on the log, shout, and when the animal stands, breathe one last deep steady time, and fire. That is how close you must be. It was all too easy.

"What you can do is go down there with your knife," Darby said. "You can slide up closer and closer, and I will do the shooting."

"Yeah, sure," Halverson said.

"Otherwise there's no point. We can shoot him right now and go home, if that's all you want, to kill a bear." She wet her index finger and marked a cross on the air. "That does it. One bear." He understood she wanted something more than he did. What did she want?

Halverson understood what he was going to do. Darby was right, this was not any kind of getting even, and making things even was not what he was about. *He didn't want me.* Those were the words of the girl who survived. As if the bear possessed some gift, and had withheld it from her.

"See if you can do it," Halverson said, and he slid a cartridge into the firing chamber, and handed the rifle to Darby. She took it like she had been waiting. Halverson gave her three cartridges. "See if you can do it," he said again.

Only when he was fifty or so yards downhill, with his skinning knife in his right hand, did Halverson wonder at all about what he was doing. He could feel the eye of the scope on his back, and as he moved carefully through the brush, Halverson thought, *now who is the hunter?*

Not even yet was he afraid. He had been afraid in the night, after dreaming, when he lay in his sleeping bag and trembled and nothing happened but the eventual sunrise. But that was gone, and nothing was left of the terrible anger he felt the first night in his cabin, if it was anger, when he heard the girl was dead. Halverson felt small and weak, but not afraid. Brilliant deep pinkish-lavender stalks of fireweed grew waist-high from long-rotted roots of an overturned alpine fir. Puffball mushrooms, over-ripe by now, clustered under them. Halverson bent and punctured the gray-white skin of a mushroom with a forefinger. It had looked like a little balloon on the ground. The skin broke; the spores rose like gunpowder smoke. The odor of the spores was that of clean earth, slightly acid, as was the taste when he licked his forefinger. Halverson felt himself touching one thing at a time with great slowness. The rasp of a wasp in the air before him was abrasive against his eyelids as he hesitated. One thing and then another. He moved carefully over the spongy lichen-covered and mossy ground between clumps of deep saw-edged grass, crouching and pushing through slowly, reaching for one of the red-purple berries that hung in clusters around him, tasting it, pulling a handful that were sticky in his palm as he crouched there eating them one at a time. The aftertaste was like a sour ache in his mouth. So, he thought, this is the way you are feeding.

Halverson stood quiet amid the buzzing of insects, listening. He heard the bear stirring just ahead in the brush. The smell of it was like an odor of clean rot in the sunlight, tangible as something to taste, the air filled with bright floating specks like infinitesimal crystalline butterflies which would settle and flutter on the tongue after drifting on currents of light. He could hear the bear's chuffing – a grunting sound which was more like slow, heavy breathing rather than anything eating. Only when he moved closer, crouching again and stepping forward slowly, did Halverson at last see the animal. Low to the ground, looking upward through leafy green brush, he saw the dark belly, and realized he was being watched. The grunting had stopped and Halverson looked up and saw the bear reared and gazing down on him, black lips curled over the fangs as though the animal were smiling, and nothing but curious.

The bear shook its head against the flies crawling on its lips in the thick juice of the berries. Halverson stepped back and stood upright, seeing that shake of the animal's head as an acknowledgment, almost a greeting. Halverson was not sure what to do except wait; he was this close, he should always have been this close. The bear lifted its muzzle, weaving its head from side to side, looking upward as if there might be some tiny thing to be seen far off in the sky, then lowered its head and dropped slowly forward, the decision made, and after a great slow bunching of itself, moved at him, hidden a moment in the brush, and then at him, before him. The leaves shook as if there had been a wind to accompany the rush. The animal stopped and reared again. Halverson lifted the knife.

With forelegs raised, the bear looked down at him. The dark eyes were soft, and the terrible odor was a stench. With the knife still upraised, Halverson waited: *this close.*

What do you do with the knife? Do you step closer, toward the embrace, and where do you plunge the blade? There was no knowing; Halverson began to move forward, stroking the blade of the knife through the air with small tentative motions while he waited to know what he should do as the bear lifted its forelegs higher, and then Halverson was no longer wondering as in the slowness of what was happening he tasted the sweet fecal breath of the animal, Halverson touching his tongue to his teeth. One thing and then another. The clean long pelt over the breast of the animal was ruffled by what had to have been a breeze in the afternoon stillness. Softly it ruffled, like a woman's hair as Halverson tried to imagine it later, except that it was really like nothing but that yellowish silver flutter before him, not like a woman's hair at all. And then there was a shot, the crack as the lead slug from the rifle broke over his head, the flat splattering sound; and Halverson saw what he had been unable to imagine, the head jerking back, the terrible involuntary slackness as the jaws gaped open, the spasm in the eyes, the flowering of blood, and the bear going down in the brush, dead with a great final rush of breath.

Halverson lowered his knife. There was nothing to defend against; there hadn't been, not unless he courted it, and the anger he felt, the trembling in his forearms, was not so much at anything as it was at loss; and he did not know what was lost. He stood over the bear, now a mere dead animal, however large, and looked at his knife. There is the least you can manage, he thought, and he dropped to his knees, enveloped in the hot stench, and began hacking, dismembering, cutting off the head. It was a long job, and he broke the knife blade prying between the vertebrae, but finally the head rolled free, a couple of turns down the slope, coming to rest beneath the clusters of red-purple berries.

When Halverson stood, his back ached and his arms and chest were sloppy from his wallowing at his job, in the blood. All the time feeling the scope on his back, Halverson rested and smoked a cigarette, and then with his arms wrapped awkwardly around it, smelling it, Halverson began transporting the head back up the slope to Darby. He wondered fleetingly if she would let him reach her. At last she lowered the rifle.

"I waited long enough, didn't I?" she asked. He stood before her, legs braced against the fleshy weight of the head. She stood on the grayish rotting log where she had rested the rifle, which she had let fall into the matted grass. Halverson set the head at her feet, so it grinned up at them – great carnivorous teeth closed and the black lips slack. He dropped the broken knife, watching it fall through the tangled grass to the mossy ground. "That will do," he said. The head of the bear could rest there on that log, the insects could have it until it was a skull, looking west.

Halverson brushed away a fly that was crawling on the fingers of his left hand. Seven cartridges were heavy in the loops of his belt. One by one he took them out and fired them away toward the peaks; the crack, the rush of the slug, then nothing. All this was one act of trust after another. The far white sky to the west was reflected from the lake below in its trough. They were inside a place where each thing irrevocably followed another, and the only hesitations were those that could be reckoned with.

Back at their camp Halverson fired the rest of his cartridges, then gave Darby the rifle and asked her to take it out and hide it in some place where it couldn't be found.

"You know that old one, that cripple the rangers killed," she said. "Well, they killed the right one. The belly was full of hair."

Halverson told her that didn't make any difference. He built a fire and sat with his back to it, watching the line of shadow rise on the peaks as the sun descended. Then he heard her coming back. "Darby," he said.

"I'm here," she said.

About the Author

William Kittredge grew up on a large desert cattle ranch in southeastern Oregon, and managed the farming operations there until 1967, when the ranch was sold. He attended the Writers' Workshop at the University of Iowa in 1968-69, and has taught creative writing at the University of Montana since 1969. He has published fiction and essays in such magazines as *Atlantic*, *Harper's*, *Rolling Stone*, *Rocky Mountain*, *Outside*, *Triquarterly*, *North American Review* and *The Iowa Review*. His current projects include a novel and a screenplay.